Ten Little Herrings

Ten Little Herrings

L.C. Tyler

FELONY & MAYHEM PRESS • NEW YORK

All the characters and events portrayed in this work are fictitious.

TEN LITTLE HERRINGS

A Felony & Mayhem mystery

PRINTING HISTORY
First UK edition (Macmillan): 2009
Felony & Mayhem edition: 2010

ISBN: 978-1-934609-52-1

Manufactured in the United States of America

Library of Congress Cataloging-in-Publication Data

Tyler, L. C.
  Ten little herrings / L.C. Tyler. -- Felony & Mayhem ed.
      p. cm.
  Originally published: London : Macmillan, 2009.
  ISBN 978-1-934609-52-1
  I. Title.
  PR6125.Y545T46 2010
  823'.92--dc22

                                    2010005200

The icon above says you're holding a book in the Felony &
Mayhem "British" category. These books are set in or around
the UK, and feature the highly literate, often witty prose that
fans of British mystery demand.

———•◦•———

For information about British titles or to learn more about
Felony & Mayhem Press, please visit us online at:

www.FelonyAndMayhem.com

Or write to us at:

Felony and Mayhem Press
156 Waverly Place
New York, NY 10014

Other "British" titles from

FELONY&MAYHEM

MICHAEL DAVID ANTHONY
The Becket Factor
Midnight Come

ROBERT BARNARD
Death on the High C's
Out of the Blackout
Death and the Chaste Apprentice
The Skeleton in the Grass
Corpse in a Gilded Cage

DUNCAN CAMPBELL
If It Bleeds

PETER DICKINSON
King and Joker
The Old English Peep Show
Skin Deep
Sleep and His Brother

CAROLINE GRAHAM
The Killings at Badger's Drift
Death of a Hollow Man
Death in Disguise
Written in Blood
Murder at Madingley Grange

CYNTHIA HARROD-EAGLES
Orchestrated Death

REGINALD HILL
A Clubbable Woman
An Advancement of Learnings
Ruling Passion
An April Shroud
A Killing Kindness
Deadheads
Death of a Dormouse

ELIZABETH IRONSIDE
Death in the Garden
The Accomplice
A Very Private Enterprise
The Art of Deception

BARRY MAITLAND
The Marx Sisters

JOHN MALCOLM
A Back Room in Somers Town

JANET NEEL
Death's Bright Angel

SHEILA RADLEY
Death in the Morning
The Chief Inspector's Daughter
A Talent for Destruction
Fate Worse than Death

L.C. TYLER
The Herring Seller's Apprentice

Ten Little Herrings

PROLOGUE

The only strange thing about my telephone conversation with Ethelred was that he had been dead for almost a year.

Well, you know how it is. You are sitting in a dead person's flat round about midnight. The Sussex rain is chucking itself against the period sash windows. A floorboard creaks, hopefully in one of the adjoining flats. The phone rings. You answer it, as you do, slightly cautiously.

'Ethelred Tressider's residence,' I said, that being the name of the dead person—though using the word 'residence' to represent Ethelred's pokey little flat was perhaps stretching the truth just a touch.

There was a long pause as if the caller had not been expecting or particularly wanting a reply.

'Zat eez zer residence of Meester Tressider?' said the caller in what can only be described as a crap accent.

'That was what I meant when I said it was Ethelred Tressider's residence,' I replied. I found this exchange strangely reassuring in the sense that a phone ringing in a cold, damp, dead-person's flat in the hush of a rural night was spooky. Finding I had a complete tosser at the other end of the line showed it was just another day at the office.

'Meester Tressider, the famous writer?'

It was the word 'famous' that made me suspicious.

'Who is that?' I asked.

There was another long pause indicating that the caller had not quite decided.

'I am sorry to trouble you, madam. It eez British Gaz,' said the voice, touchingly pleased with itself. 'I just want to check if Meester Tressider's thermostat eez set at an appropriate temperature for zer winter.'

'Ethelred?' I said. 'That's you, isn't it?'

This time the voice did not hesitate.

'No,' it said. 'Is British Gaz. Complimentary safety check.'

'At midnight?'

'So sorry, memsahib. It is not midnight at the call centre. In Bangalore we are all working so very hard.'

Actually (I do know where Bangalore is) it would have been around 5 a.m., but that wasn't what gave it away.

'Why has your accent changed from German to Welsh?' I asked.

'Not Welsh, Indian. In Bangalore we are all so, so Indian. Please can you confirm Mr Tressider's thermostat has been correctly adjusted for your English winter.'

'Ethelred, stop pissing about,' I said, on the grounds that one of us needed to come to the point. 'The thermostat is just fine for a dead person's flat. If you think you may not be dead, I'll set it a notch or two higher. Now, you dim tart, where exactly are you?'

'Dead?' said the voice. There was a note of concern there that was not entirely central heating related. It was at that point that I remembered that news of his death might not have reached him. That was something I was going to have to explain to him in due course—and preferably in much more coherent fashion than

I am now explaining it to you. Oh...and I'd killed him, by the way. Yes, it was going to take some careful explaining at some point.

Ethelred Tressider, for I was sure that it was he, would have made a better job of telling the story. As an obscure yet experienced crime writer, he knew all about plotting, characterisation, pacing and so on and so forth. He would not have had a phone call from a dead person on page one and the accidental revelation of the killer on page two. As an obscure yet experienced crime writer he would still have been carefully setting the scene, explaining who everyone was. He would not have plunged randomly into the story leaving the readers to follow or not as they preferred. And, as an obscure but experienced crime writer, he was going to be pretty pissed off to discover I had killed him.

An apology was probably called for.

'Ethelred, you dickhead,' I said, 'You realise this is entirely your fault?'

'All Mr Tressider's fault?' the voice now sounded hurt as well as Welsh.

'Let's cut to the chase, shall we? Where are you Ethelred? I need to know...for certain reasons that I shall explain when I see you.'

'Bangalore,' said the voice, making one last pathetic attempt to convince itself.

'That's Bangalore, Cardiganshire?'

'I am not knowing what is Cardiganshire.'

'*Nos da*,' I said.

'*Nos da*,' said the voice sadly.

And I hung up. Well, if he wanted to play silly buggers, I'd leave him to stew for a while.

Of course, the moment I hung up I regretted it. After all, I'd waited almost a year for this call—those strange eleven months since Ethelred had died so tragically and improbably at my hands.

Now that he was back in contact, I was forced to re-examine my motives for doing what I had done. It wasn't jealousy exactly.

I really am not the jealous type of girl, as you well know. Ethelred was nothing to me and, while I am sure that he lusted after my size 12 (some labels anyway) figure, I was probably nothing to him either. But the fact remained that he had chosen to desert me and fly off to re-join his Floozy: the Scarlet Woman whose name will never be typed by my fingers. You could argue that all middle-aged writers are entitled to one floozy. But she was the wrong floozy *for him*. Honestly. It really had been kinder to kill Ethelred there and then.

A creaking floorboard and another sudden death-rattle from the aged sash window brought me back to the here and now. I listened to a series of thumps, then silence reigned again in West Sussex. Was somebody's dodgy prostate causing them to take a midnight trip to the bathroom? I reminded myself that I did not believe in ghosts, not even ghosts of technically dead crime writers.

What I needed to do was track Ethelred down and sort all this out. Explain to him in what senses he was dead and, to look on the bright side, in what senses he was alive. Explain to him in which (minor) ways it might be my fault and in which ways it was definitely entirely his fault. Amid all of this confusion, what I had to do was to focus on some hard facts and figures. The figure that immediately came to mind was fifteen percent (twenty five percent film, foreign and translation rights). Yes, that was the one thing that I could be certain of. Dead or alive, I was still Ethelred's agent.

CHAPTER 1

I haven't always been an agent.

When I was young, I wanted to be a vet. I liked the idea of looking after creatures with minimal intelligence who needed somebody to sweep up after them. I wanted to spend my time with lower forms of life that were incapable of answering me back. It didn't take me long to work out my true vocation in life.

The Elsie Thirkettle Agency quickly attracted a number of promising young authors of high literary merit, but I managed to dump most of them. It's a question of quantity, not quality, you see. The agricultural revolution was all about getting two crops a year out of a field that previously gave you one. It's much the same with books. The royalties on a book that has taken five years to produce are usually pretty much the same as on one written in six months. I can double-, sometimes treble-, crop my authors. There were a number of laws that I was able to formulate:

1. Elsie's First Law—Get the manuscript out of their grubby little hands the moment they hit the required

number of words. A second draft will be better in some ways but it will certainly be much worse in others. Just send it to a publisher and let the nice editor do the rest. Do by all means check first that it is actually a different plot from the previous book—but see Elsie's Second Law.

2. Elsie's Second Law—Always get them to write a sequel if they know how. After all, they've got the characters. They've checked out the locations. They've hooked a few unwitting punters. It's true that producing sequels is a sure sign of the second-rate author but, then again, see Elsie's Third Law.

3. Elsie's Third Law—Books by second- or even third-rate authors cost as much as books by first-rate authors. This is odd, when you think about it. It's a bit like charging the same for mink as for fake nylon fur on the grounds that it's still a coat. Or charging the same for Lafitte as for red plonk. Or charging the same for good and bad chocolate (though, obviously, there is no such thing as bad chocolate). You wouldn't think you could do it, but see Elsie's Fourth Law.

4. Elsie's Fourth Law—It's amazing what you can get away with.

Ethelred was one of my successes. In the early days he hankered after prizes and critical acclaim but, once I had explained things to him properly, I could get at least two, sometimes three or four, books a year under a variety of pen names. He wrote mainly detective stories but he also wrote romantic fiction. What gave his romances such poignancy was,

I think, his long and consistent experience of being dumped by a variety of women, and repeatedly by his (ex) wife. He deserved better. Not me necessarily, but somebody very much like me.

Then he hit some sort of mid-life crisis and decided to clear off with the Scarlet Woman (whose name will never etc etc) without telling me a thing until he was safely out of the country. It was only right that, some time later, I should have not consulted him over his death.

I might have believed he had intended to vanish permanently had he not left painstakingly detailed instructions with me for the maintenance of his boiler while he was away. He was the sort of crime writer who worries a lot about his boiler.

As his literary agent I was of course not only responsible for his boiler. In his absence, I paid his bills, opened any of his mail that looked interesting, transferred his royalties (less reasonable agency deductions) to his account and checked his bank and credit card statements for any clue as to where he was or what he was doing. I also visited the flat from time to time to ensure all was well and to reassure his neighbours that he was still travelling to research his next novel. Very occasionally (because it was a long journey back) I stayed over. Actually it wasn't really that far back to Hampstead but, when I was in the flat, reassuringly surrounded by his shapeless tweedy jackets, his tatty old Barbour and his green wellies, it was easier to believe that his absence was merely the temporary aberration that I was telling people it was.

The bank statements and the rest of it, however, pointed to the reverse. Financially he was flat-lining. No indication of life at all. In my case, my credit card statement is one of my vital signs—when it goes blank, you'll know I'm dead. But Ethelred could survive for months on a bowl of rice and an organic muesli bar. He selected his clothes purely for their durability. It didn't follow that lack of spending meant it was time to close the case.

Obviously, it was worth getting him back if at all possible, but there are no handbooks for recovering missing authors—no tips on the Internet. You don't get ads in the local papers—missing dogs, yes; missing authors, no. It doesn't seem to be something people want to do that much.

Then it struck me. He had not needed to use his credit card or cash card so far because he had access to cash from somewhere. But sooner or later, in my experience, cash runs out. Then he would need plastic. If I waited until the relevant credit card statement came in, I would know where he had used it; but that only meant I could be certain where he was *last* month. On the other hand if I cancelled all his cards…

I can't claim it was the work of a moment. Card companies tend to want to speak to the owner of the card, but if you convince them that you've just lost somebody's card that they left with you, and you think the card and PIN number may have fallen into the hands of bad people with expensive tastes, then you can panic them into a bit of action. In twenty minutes Ethelred was, tragically, credit-less.

I sat back to await another phone call.

It came within a fortnight.

In the interim I had been speculating on where Ethelred might be. The Loire Valley was where he liked to spend his holidays, staying in hotels with peeling wallpaper, drinking obscure wines and confirming every Frenchman's prejudice about the Englishman abroad. That of course was too obvious to be a real possibility. Clearly he was not in Bangalore. He disliked Benidorm, Corfu or anywhere else that attracted crowds of his fellow countrymen in large numbers. That left most of the rest of the world, which is big. I was still undecided, right up to the moment the call came.

It was nine in the evening when the novelty frog phone started singing Greensleeves, this time in my flat in Hampstead.

I silenced the frog in mid verse by lifting the receiver. 'Elsie Thirkettle,' I said.

'Did you cancel my cards?'

'Why should I do that?'

'I have no idea. I am not really interested in why you did it. I just asked: *did* you?'

'You just cleared off and left me,' I said, mustering some righteous indignation. 'How was I to know whether you were supposed to be dead or alive? A phone call would have been good. Even a postcard would have been better than nothing.'

'I phoned you two weeks ago.'

'No, that was British Gas. Remember?'

There was, strangely, no reply to that.

'Why couldn't you just have the normal sort of mid-life crisis,' I continued. 'Why couldn't you buy a Harley-Davison, join a heavy metal band, find religion? Why did it have to involve vanishing without trace? With Her?'

There was a long sigh. 'It seemed like a good idea at the time.'

'And now?'

'And now I'd like my credit cards back. Please.'

'Where are you exactly, Ethelred?' I asked.

There was a pause. 'Abroad,' he said with more caution than was really called for.

'In that case, this call must be costing you a bit,' I said.

There was another pause. 'I hadn't really thought,' he said.

'Well, think now and get to the point.'

'I need you to get my cards working again.'

'Only you can do that.'

'Great. Who do I phone?'

'It's not quite that simple,' I said.

'Not quite that simple?'

'They need you to go into the bank in person to clear one or two things up.'

'One or two things?'

'Let's say up to about six.'

'Have you done something stupid?'

'No,' I said, but I was lying.

'So what do I do now?'

'If you ever want to use plastic again, you'll need to come back to England.'

There was a long sigh. 'Can you phone my hotel then and pay the bill with your own card so that I can leave?'

'No.'

'But...' said the card-less person.

'I'm not paying your bill so you can wander off with some floozy,' I pointed out. 'You're hopeless with women. I'm coming to collect you. Where do I have to get a plane to?'

'There are no more women in my life—and certainly no floozies. As for planes, you'll need to come to Tours, I suppose, if you want to fly. But it's probably easier to get the train. I'm in the Loire Valley—to be exact I'm at the Vieille Auberge in Chaubord. It's right opposite the chateau. You can't miss it.'

'Does it happen to have any peeling wallpaper?'

'Yes. It's the only sort of wallpaper it has.'

'Does it smell of mildew and old cheese?'

'Yes. Both.'

'Is there anywhere else to stay?'

'Quite possibly, but this is where I am staying. I like it.'

'Then book me a room for tomorrow night,' I said.

'Just one night?'

'I can't see why we should need to stay longer,' I said. I figured we needed to stay long enough for me to explain what I had done and for him to understand why it had been for his own good.

Of course, I had no way of knowing that, in a hotel full of stamp collectors, the guests would suddenly start murdering each other. It's not the sort of thing you usually plan for, is it?

CHAPTER 2

Ethelred met me at the station. He came dressed, for some reason, as the Englishman Abroad. He wore a crumpled linen suit, a crumpled stripy tie and a panama hat. It would have looked eccentric at any time but at a provincial railway station on a cold, rainy December afternoon it attracted many admiring glances.

'Ethelred, you prat,' I said, standing on tiptoe to kiss him on the lower part of both cheeks. 'Why are you wearing fancy dress?'

'It's all I've got,' he said. 'You cancelled my cards, remember?'

'You must have other clothes. It's been too cold for this sort of get-up for months.'

'Not where I've been.'

'Which was?'

'I told you: India.'

'You were *actually* working in a British Gas call centre in Bangalore?'

'I may have made some of it up,' he conceded, looking over the top of my head. (He's just a fraction taller than I am.) 'I was in fact in Goa when I phoned you,' he added, as if that proved something.

'Good for you,' I said.

'I have been to Bangalore,' he added.

'Do you have any idea just how little I care where you went with that tart?'

'Yes,' he said.

'Good. So when did you get here?' I asked.

He shrugged. 'A few days ago.'

'Best get you back to Sussex then,' I said.

He nodded meekly. 'What I don't understand, though,' he said, 'is why you keep telling me I'm dead. What exactly have you done, Elsie?'

I thought of the exploding plane and, for just a second, felt something that was a bit like remorse. I realised that sooner or later I was going to have to own up. I therefore drew myself up to my full height and said: 'I suppose you don't know where I could get some chocolate round here, do you?'

It was, after all, a genuine emergency. I'd forgotten to buy chocolate before leaving St Pancras, and after five hours travelling I was starting to get cold sweats, trembling hands and blurred vision.

'There is in fact a *chocolaterie* in town,' he said. 'It's called Apollinaire. I'm told it's very good.'

'I'll drop my bag at the hotel first,' I said. 'Then guide me to Apollinaire.'

Ethelred took my bag, like the gent he is, and we set off on what he claimed was a short walk to the hotel. They had however put the town centre on the wrong side of the river from the railway station, and cold wind was blowing down the Loire. Conversation was minimal until we had crossed the bridge.

'Did you bring any English newspapers with you?' he eventually asked, the perennial question of the Englishman abroad.

Actually they had given me one on Eurostar, but I'd dumped it in a bin at the Gare du Nord. Still, I was able to fill him in on the main stories that I thought a crime writer might appreciate.

'There's been a jewellery robbery in London,' I said. 'A big haul of diamonds. Then there was that company that was taken over by that other company—the Russian one?—well, the pension fund is in a complete mess and the pensioners have been left high and dry. I suppose that's not really crime though? I mean, they're allowed to do that aren't they?'

I paused. Ethelred just nodded vaguely, meaning either they were or they weren't or that he couldn't give monkey's.

'Oh yes,' I went on. 'There was another good crime story. Somebody is trying to blackmail this fizzy drink company. They say they've got the secret recipe for their cola and will publish it on the Internet if the company doesn't pay up. Sorry—I forgot—you don't know what the Internet is, do you?'

Ethelred shrugged again, showing that he did speak some French, and said: 'Football results?'

'Tottenham Wednesday beat Manchester something...' I said. Or was that cricket? 'Where is this hotel exactly?'

'We're almost there. You can see those lights ahead of us. Right opposite the chateau. Any news on the literary front?'

'Yes, your last novel was spoken of as a serious contender for the Booker Prize.'

'Was it?' he said, brightening up.

'As if,' I said. You would think that writers would spot irony, wouldn't you?

I racked my brains for anything else that might amuse him. 'There was something on this ten kroner puce they've discovered.'

That was an interesting story, in its way, and not without its own little ironies. It concerned a small pink piece of paper with tatty white perforations, originating in Denmark. Until recently there had been only one of these stamps in the world—sold in Denmark some time in the eighteen fifties, when ten kroner would have been enough to post an elephant from Odense to Aarhus and back. They apparently never needed that many of them. Being the only such stamp surviving, it had been worth a bit more than ten kroner. The bad news for its owner was that a collector in Nykøbing (F) had come across two more in his attic. The pink stamp had thus ceased to be part of that exclusive and highly prized club of single known specimens. On the mere rumour of other stamps of a similar colour and price, its re-sale value had plummeted overnight—to a paltry million dollars or thereabouts. There were hints that the newly discovered stamps had to be fakes. This was only the beginning of the story however, because the stamps had then vanished again. The owner had died and the family, who had always regarded Uncle Peter's interest in philately as a bit of a waste of time and didn't read the relevant magazines, decided to clear the house before selling it. It was only after Uncle Peter's heirs had been contacted by a number of solicitous but very interested stamp dealers that they checked the will and remembered a couple of albums and several bags of assorted stamps that they had sold off at a flea market. They could not recall, offhand, whether two of the stamps had been pink, though they rather thought they might have been. The family were, as the saying goes, well gutted.

Conversely, somebody out there was probably quite pleased—since the stamps had gone for a mere five kroner per bag—scarcely enough to pay the postage on an ivory tooth-pick travelling from one side of Copenhagen to the other. There was speculation that, if the seller of the stamps discovered exactly who had them, they might try to recover them through the courts—though what their case was, other than their own stupidity, was not immediately apparent.

Strangely, this one did interest Ethelred in the sense that he let out another of his long sighs. 'There's been talk of nothing else here at the hotel,' he said.

Since we were not in Nykøbing, this was mildly surprising.

'There's a stamp fair going on at the chateau,' he explained wearily. 'Actually it finished today, but most of the people staying at the hotel since I arrived have been stamp collectors or stamp dealers. Occasionally they talk about stamps. At breakfast. At lunch. At dinner. In the lounge. In the bar. In the corridors. I fear for their souls.'

'You can go to Hell for talking about stamps?' I asked.

'I hope so,' said Ethelred devoutly.

But the stamp people did not in fact only talk about stamps. In the hotel reception I met a nice Russian stamp collector, named Grigory Davidov. He was a little plumper than his doctor might have liked and more than a little pleased with himself—but he did have a very sound knowledge of chocolate.

'Apollinaire!' he said reverently, having overheard me talking to Ethelred. 'Whatever you do, make sure you buy some of the peach truffles. They are *divine.*' He did a sort of slobbery kissy thing with his fat fingers and his fat lips. I made a mental note to cut down a fraction on chocolate if I ever thought I might be putting on that sort of weight, though I reckon if you're my build you can carry a few extra pounds without it noticing.

'Peach truffles?' I repeated in reverential tones.

'They are all good, naturally—the fondants, the violet creams, the champagne truffles—but I invariably select a peach truffle from the box first,' he said. 'The first chocolate from a full box is a sacred moment, do you not agree?'

I nodded. This is so true.

'Of course they are not so good for the figure,' said Davidov with a throaty chuckle.

'You look well on it,' I lied.

'With my build I can carry a few extra pounds without it noticing,' he said with a modest smile.

Call me stupid, but I only bought a small box of assorted truffles to begin with. I'd eaten half of them before I got back to the hotel.

And they were indeed very, very good. Still, I could always get some more tomorrow before we checked out.

And call me a little over-focused on cocoa-based confectionary, but it was not until I had restored chocolate levels in my body that I remembered that I had not answered Ethelred's question. Why did I keep going on about his death? Yes, I would certainly need to explain.

But, the way I saw it, that could all wait for a bit. Anyway, plenty of authors were worth more dead than alive. It would be fine.

CHAPTER 3

Elsie was right, as always.

If I was going to have a mid-life crisis, then it might as well have been a conventional one, and my choice of companion had been ill-advised. By the time I phoned Elsie for help I had been humiliated and abandoned. I am, of course, well used to humiliation; the only novelty was experiencing it in India. On reflection, I have to say that humiliation in India felt much the same as it had in Oxford, London and Sussex. It is certainly not worth going there for that purpose alone. Trust me on that.

And yet it had all started so well a year before.

With a single bound, or so it seemed to me, I was free. As a writer I have always tried to avoid the more obvious clichés, but that was how it felt as I scurried with my bags away from the short-term car park and towards the terminal building, leaving Elsie in my car, sleeping off the effects of a slightly drugged mug of drinking chocolate. I was free as a person, free as a writer. Elsie had for some time been telling me to get a life. I was simply following her instructions, as I had so many times before. She just hadn't envisaged my drugging her so that I could make an unimpeded getaway.

What she did not know, moreover, was that I had been planning this for a while. My airline tickets were in my pocket. I had a wallet full of untraceable cash that would, with luck, keep me going for a while. I had left adequate instructions for the maintenance of my boiler. I was a free spirit at last.

As I glanced through one of the vast plate-glass windows on my way to the departure lounge, I saw that the sun was rising. It was rising only over Hounslow, admittedly, but it symbolised other dawns in other places, whose names I could as yet only guess at.

'Have a pleasant flight, sir,' said the young lady as she handed me back my boarding pass.

'You bet your ass, kid,' I responded.

And for a while it was good. It really was. I (and my 'floozy' as Elsie insists on calling her) wandered barefoot along the dazzlingly white sand of a number of lonely beaches; we watched the burning sunset sky (and, just occasionally, the burning sunrise sky) over pink coral reefs; sometimes we lost ourselves in the contemplation of distant blue hills; sometimes we found strange, abandoned temples, half hidden in the deep shadows of banana groves on the edge of viridian paddy fields. One night we would sleep in creamy, silk sheets at the most expensive hotel in Singapore, an empty Champagne bottle resting at the end of the four-poster bed; the next, we would be in a shack on the beach somewhere in Sumatra, with the soft tropical moonlight slanting in through the broken shutters onto our shared mat. Another time, we slept on faded red cushions on the deck of a dhow that we had hired by the day and ate chubby, rose-coloured fish, which we had caught on lines and which we barbequed on bleached driftwood on a tiny, rocky island in the Indian Ocean. We ate excellent steak in a run-down eating-house in the red light district of Jakarta, and casually exchanged views on the painted girls and their clients as they passed through. We travelled by mule along narrow paths and stayed some weeks in a monastery in a hidden valley in the Himalayas, where we woke every morning to tea laced with rancid butter and to the sight of a thin, clean wisp of cloud, streaming off the summit of Annapurna in the bright blue above us. We supplemented the cash I had brought with me with her own more extensive ill-gotten gains. Nothing was planned. Everything was done on a whim. Then, on a whim no doubt, one morning I found myself alone. She had gone and, it appeared, my remaining cash had elected to go with her. For the cash it was going to be a short life, but it would be a happy one.

I spent the day strolling barefoot along the beach to show myself that I could be a free spirit perfectly well on my own. Later I bought myself a pair of socks. That evening I decided that I had better check that all was well with my boiler in Sussex.

I had no wish to contact Elsie yet, but it seemed to me that if I phoned my old number and the phone was working then bills were being paid and all was probably well generally. If the phone had been cut off then Elsie had not forgiven me and it was time to fly home and sort out the frozen pipes.

I tried to work out the time difference between India and West Sussex. I had no wish to wake everyone in the block of flats with the phone ringing in the middle of the night. Unfortunately I miscalculated. Even more unfortunately—and quite inexplicably—it was Elsie who answered the phone.

'Ethelred Tressider's residence,' she said, in a manner that can be described only as 'proprietorial'. What on earth was she doing there?

For a moment I was not sure what to say, and then I came up with a brilliant idea.

'Is that the residence of Mr Ethelred Tressider?' I asked in a cleverly assumed accent.

'That was what I meant when I said it was Ethelred Tressider's residence,' said a tired voice at the other end. 'Who is that?'

'I am sorry to trouble you, madam,' I said, 'It is British Gas. I just want to check if Mr Tressider's thermostat is set at an appropriate temperature for the winter.'

'Ethelred?' she said. 'That's you, isn't it?'

This was obviously a lucky guess on Elsie's part, but I was having none of it. I told her it was a complimentary safety check.

'At midnight?'

Midnight? I checked my watch again and recalculated. So, London was *behind* India then?

'So sorry, memsahib,' I said, slipping subtly into an Indian accent. 'It is not midnight at the call centre. Please can you confirm Mr Tressider's thermostat has been correctly adjusted for the winter?'

'Ethelred, stop pissing about. The thermostat is just fine for a dead person's flat. If you think you may not be dead, I'll set it a notch or two higher. Now, you dim tart, where exactly are you?'

'Dead?' I said. This was news to me. What was Elsie playing at? My plan was to disappear and start a new life. Dying was never intended to be part of it. I wondered if I had misheard.

'Ethelred, you dickhead,' she said suddenly and inexplicably, 'You realise this is entirely your fault?'

For a moment I almost forgot who I wasn't, but recollected myself sufficiently to say: 'All *Mr Tressider's* fault?' But I was still trying to work out what other words sounded like 'dead'.

'Let's cut to the chase, shall we?' Elsie was saying. 'Where are you Ethelred? I need to know…for certain reasons that I shall explain when I see you.'

'Bangalore,' I said. I'd been there recently.

'That's Bangalore, Cardiganshire?'

The game was clearly up, but that did not stop me blundering onwards. 'I am not knowing what is Cardiganshire,' I said.

'*Nos da,*' she said in a voice heavily laden with sarcasm.

'*Nos da,*' I replied stupidly.

And the phone went dead—a bit as I had myself, it would seem. It was clear that Elsie had done something idiotic, but what exactly? If she had had me legally declared dead, then my passport would have been cancelled, so it wasn't that that she meant. Whatever it was, it was clearly worse than that. But what *was* worse than that? I had no doubt I would find out soon enough.

I opened the bedroom window and listened for a while to the deafening trill of the cicadas. In the distance I heard the surf washing against the still-warm sand. The humid Indian night caressed my face and I breathed in a smell that was spices and drains in approximately equal measure. I had thought this was my future, but it was starting to look like my past. I closed the window again, switched the air-conditioning up to full blast and, tugging the sheet up over my head, tried to sleep.

A fortnight later I was in a reasonably-priced hotel in the Loire Valley and all of my credit cards had been cancelled.

As mid-life crises go, this one was turning out to be a bit of a disappointment.

CHAPTER 4

We were sitting in the hotel restaurant when Ethelred finished his account of his time in India and elsewhere. It sounded a bit rubbish. I blamed him mostly but (to be fair) I blamed Her mostly as well.

'A postcard would have been nice,' I reminded him. 'Or didn't it bother you that I might have thought you were dead.'

'This thing about my being dead...' he began.

Sooner or later I was going to have to face up to this one. Now wasn't a bad time, but I felt sure there would be better. Yes, indeed.

'And in the meantime who was looking after your boiler?' I demanded.

'I am of course immensely grateful. Now about my death...'

'Grateful? So you should be. You owe me for a full service, by the way.'

'I assume the royalties are still coming in on my novels,' he said.

I nodded. 'You are still selling a few. It's time you completed another one of your Inspector Fairfax novels. Your publisher is quite keen.'

Ethelred shook his head.

'They were offering to increase your royalty on the first ten thousand by half a percent.'

'I'm not doing any more Fairfax,' he said. 'I thought I might try something new—a hardboiled police procedural, set somewhere nobody has used yet.'

'Not Edinburgh, then?' I said.

'Not Edinburgh. I thought maybe Brighton, and with a younger main character...'

'And a taste for Mozart, no doubt.'

'I thought Boccherini, perhaps,' he said.

'Not well enough known,' I said.

'He's pretty well known.'

'Not to your readers.'

'Some of my loyal readers will have heard of him.'

'Ethelred, *neither* of your loyal readers will have heard of him. Mozart's safer. Trust me.'

Ethelred wasn't too happy with this so I asked him (as you do) whether he was working on something at this moment.

'I completed another manuscript just before I left,' Ethelred said slightly sheepishly.

'Did you?' I asked. I don't think my face showed any trace of guilt. It doesn't usually.

'I assumed you would have found it and read it,' Ethelred continued.

'Did you?' I asked. (See note on guilt.)

'It's fine if you didn't,' he went on. 'It contained some fairly personal stuff that I clearly needed to get out of my system. I'm a bit relieved if you didn't see it. On reflection, it's not something I'd want published.'

'Isn't it?' I asked.

'No,' he said.

I was just wondering how to reply when the waiter appeared and handed us some menus. Ethelred immediately busied himself with selecting an hors-d'œuvre and an entrée. I went straight to the desserts and made a short-list of four.

Ethelred had by this stage moved on to the wine list, and

was frowning as his finger worked its way down the page. In the absence of grown-up conversation, I contented myself by looking round the room at our fellow guests. The hotel still contained, as Ethelred had warned me, a number of philatelists of various shapes and sizes, few of them attractive. I mentioned this to Ethelred. He reluctantly disengaged himself from the wine list.

'The place was much fuller last night,' he said. 'A lot of people will have checked out today, of course, now that the stamp fair is over. This really is the end of the season. The receptionist was saying that it will be just him on duty tonight. There are only twelve guests remaining in the hotel. By tomorrow evening it will be more or less empty.'

I surveyed what was clearly now just the last dregs of a stamp fair. The dining room must have seemed cavernous even when full. At one end was a giant stone fireplace of a type that could conceivably have been popular in the Middle Ages. Its upper portions were dominated by a grand coat of arms, to which the hotel owner might or might not have been entitled. In the hearth a purely token log fire smouldered fitfully. From a beamed ceiling, painted an improbable shade of red, hung several rustic chandeliers. It called for a large and jovial gathering of lords, ladies, peasants, troubadours and huntsmen. But, sadly, it had us.

The nice (if plump) Mr Davidov was over on the far side, alone but happy, chomping down on a large plate of cassoulet. He wiped his mouth with his napkin and waved a podgy hand in my direction. A weasely little man was at the table next to him, sipping the smallest size of beer that the restaurant served and reading a stamp magazine in an ostentatious manner. His clothing suggested that he considered Oxfam to be a designer label. A good wash might have given the beige trousers respectability, but only a time-machine could have made the chocolate-brown top fashionable. On the plus side, assuming he had cut his hair himself that morning in poor light and using nail scissors, then he hadn't made such a bad job of it. Observing the trajectory of Mr Davidov's greeting, the weasel's attention was diverted briefly in my direction. He studied me briefly and then returned, with a slight sneer, to his philatelic studies. One table further along was a tall, actually rather good looking, young stamp collector with dark black hair, on whom my gaze necessarily lingered slightly longer. He looked a bit like a film star—to be exact, a bit like the sort of film star who would play the sympathetic, reliable friend of the kooky main character, who (since it is clearly the kooky main character who is going to end up with Cameron Diaz) might just be available for *you*. He looked like the nice sort of boy you could take home to your mother, though you'd probably want to try other stuff with him first. I gave him a wink to show that he'd pulled, but he obviously did not see it, and he failed to look in my direction for the rest of the evening. Then there were a couple of quite blatant, balding philatelists, in tweed jackets even Ethelred would have sent to the charity shop. It was an almost entirely male company and mainly quite middle-aged. The only obvious non-collectors were a German family close to us—mother, father, son, daughter, mainly blond, all chattering away. I did a quick tally and made that eleven, not twelve, including Ethelred and me—so somebody had miscounted.

I switched my attention back to the young man with dark hair. He was still looking in the wrong direction, but I undid another button of my blouse, just in case.

'They have a Chenonceau on the list,' Ethelred said, looking up at last. 'By the way, your button has come undone. The Chenonceau is quite rare but, unlike stamps, that does not make it expensive.'

He gave a little chuckle at his joke. I shrugged. Wine is wine and Ethelred (though I hadn't told him yet) was paying for dinner. It was all much the same to me. There was chocolate torte on the menu. The evening would not therefore be totally in vain.

Had I needed any confirmation as to what my choice of dessert was going to be, then I received it half way through my main course. Mr Davidov waddled up to our table. He was smartly but casually dressed in a leather jacket, plain grey shirt, capacious and well-pressed blue Armani jeans and an IWC Grande Complication—a watch that makes a plain old Rolex look a bit cheap. He seemed to be making the point that he was Russian New Money in much the same way that Ethelred's shapeless linen jacket made the point that he was English distressed gentry—not a good plan in either case. Davidov smiled genially.

'I have,' he said, 'just been to the kitchen to congratulate the chef on his torte. It is really excellent.'

'A personal visit?' said Ethelred. 'It was too good then to just send your compliments via the waiter?' The words were innocent enough, but there was an edge to them—a suggestion that Davidov was being a little pretentious. If so, the suggestion rolled off Davidov like water from a (fat) Labrador's coat.

Davidov fingered the soft leather of his jacket and smiled. 'I find that kitchen staff are so appreciative of a personal visit,' he smiled. 'I also congratulated them last night on their soufflé.'

'Really? That's thoughtful of you,' said Ethelred. Again, the words were unexceptional but the note of antagonism was obvious to anyone with the slightest sensitivity. Perhaps it was just that our food was getting cold as we chatted. Ethelred pointedly took a pinch of salt and aimed it roughly in the direction of his food. Most of it missed the plate.

'That is unlucky,' said Davidov, eyeing the tablecloth. 'To spill salt, I mean.'

'You are superstitious?' asked Ethelred.

'All Russians are superstitious,' said Davidov.

'I'm not,' said Ethelred. 'And there's plenty more salt where that came from.'

Davidov simply grinned, winked at me and whispered: 'chocolate torte, *Madame.*' He bowed very formally to Ethelred and went on his way.

'You don't like him much, do you?' I asked.

'I have no views one way or the other,' said Ethelred huffily.

I did not pursue it. To the extent I had a view, I too doubted that the chef welcomed kitchen visits by random hotel guests at the busiest time of the evening. But my mind was already focusing on obscenely rich chocolate cake, so these thoughts did not detain me long.

We had scarcely drunk our coffee before Ethelred announced that he wanted an early night, leaving me with the choice of wandering the freezing streets looking for an emergency 24-hour chocolate dispensary or heading for the bar. The sight of a nice boy, whom I could take in due course to meet my mother, moving bar-wards convinced me that I needed a little nightcap. Since Ethelred had blown the chance of an evening in my company, I felt free to turn my attentions elsewhere.

I followed at a discreet distance, got myself a Perrier and nonchalantly wandered over to the only occupied table.

'Is there room here for a small one?' I asked.

He looked blank and then said: 'Oh, you mean you.'

I confirmed that was what I meant. He looked round at the five empty tables elsewhere in the bar and shrugged. I joined him at his table, smoothing my skirt slowly as I sat.

'Elsie Thirkettle,' I said, skirt adjustments complete. I held out my hand.

'Jonathan Gold,' he replied, as if his attention was elsewhere.

My hand was still hovering in mid air. He seemed disinclined to shake it or do anything else with it. I put it away for later.

'Nice evening,' I said.

'Is it?'

Well, possibly not. It was the middle of winter, after all. I realised he was now looking over my shoulder and turned to see what competition I had. It was just the weasely individual, still improbably clutching his small beer. He took a seat at one of the empty tables.

'A friend?' I asked conversationally.

'I've seen him before,' said Gold.

Since they had been staying at the same hotel, this seemed likely. I pointed that out.

'No—before I came here,' said Gold, a little irritably. He lapsed into a contemplative silence. This was not good.

I decided it was time to show we had shared interests. I therefore did my best to remember the details of the Danish stamp story.

'You'll be pretty excited about this ten kroner puce thingy,' I said.

'What's that?' he asked. He glanced over my shoulder again, but this time I did not turn round. I needed to focus his attention on me.

'It's a stamp,' I said. When talking to Ethelred earlier it had all been fairly fresh in my mind, but, a few hours on, my brain had discarded all the bits of the story that it did not require long-term. 'It's a pink stamp.'

'You collect them, do you?' he asked.

'I'm fascinated by them,' I said. This seemed to be the right thing to say in order to pull a really fit stamp collector.

He shrugged.

'Maybe it's not the sort of thing you collect?' I said. I was aware that serious stamp-heads didn't just grab everything they could lay their hands on and gum them in.

'What colour did you say?' asked Gold.

'Puce.'

'Sounds revolting.'

'You *are* here for the stamp fair?' I asked.

'Yes—it's just not the sort of thing I collect,' he said. He seemed a little distant, but he would soon be putty in my hands.

'And what *do* you collect?' I asked sweetly, cupping my chin in my hands and fluttering my eyelashes.

I was expecting him to name a country or period or (could that possibly be right?) a colour. I hoped he might say: 'Actually I collect babes like you, when my luck is really in.' But he just said: 'Let's get this straight. You're a friend of Davidov's aren't you?'

'Not a friend exactly,' I replied, though obviously there is an affinity between all chocolate lovers. In a very real sense Grigory Davidov and I were chocolate buddies. 'You might say that we share a similar view of the world.'

'You approve of Davidov?'

'He seems to be right on the important issues,' I said with a smile. The smile was not returned.

'How can you side with that bloated oligarch?' asked Gold.

That's the trouble these days. One small square of chocolate, a few extra inches round the waist, and you're automatically some sort of food criminal. It's sad. Though deep down I still had plans for young Gold to rip my clothes off with his teeth, I drew myself up to my full height and said: 'OK, I may not be entirely politically correct but I honestly think that Mr Davidov has excellent taste...'

Not exactly conciliatory, I grant you, but I wasn't expecting him to stand up and say: 'You make me want to vomit.'

I would have said something clever in response but he had gone before I had taken it all in. And even after he had gone I couldn't think of anything clever to say. As hot dates go, that had to be the seventh or eighth worst I had ever had.

But a nastier date was on offer within moments.

'May I join you?'

The weasely-faced stamp enthusiast had edged silently across from his table to mine. Close up his trousers looked a little more stained than from a distance, but otherwise he was much as expected.

'If you must,' I said—a bit ungraciously, but I'm not usually told by attractive young men that I have emetic qualities and was trying to work out what I was supposed to have said.

'I see that you have a drink already,' he said with a nod towards my Perrier. No need for him to buy me one then. Well, *he* certainly knew how to show a girl a good time.

'Yup,' I said, absent-mindedly, still wondering how I had spooked the only decent man in the hotel (crime writers excepted).

'You have been talking to Mr Davidov and to Mr Gold,' he observed.

'Briefly,' I said.

'Both of them?'

'Spot on,' I said. He wasn't proving to be much of a conversationalist either.

He looked at me more closely than my own reply would seem to justify. 'Are you a collector or a dealer?' he asked.

'Neither. I'm an agent.'

He frowned, as though trying to fit me into the world of stamp collecting. He couldn't. 'And you are working for...?'

I looked him up and down and decided I wouldn't be asking him to rip my clothes off with his teeth, at least not tonight.

'I'm here with Mr Tressider,' I said.

'And what is your relationship with him?'

'Purely business,' I said, a little primly perhaps.

He nodded.

'So, what's your role, exactly?' he asked.

I wondered whether to explain in detail what a literary agent did.

'The way I see it,' I said, 'I've been sent to keep Mr Tressider on the straight and narrow. And, right now, to ensure he gets safely back to London.'

He looked puzzled, and then the light seemed to dawn. 'Then it could be we have more in common than I thought. Perhaps we could continue this discussion in my room? Where we won't be disturbed?'

'In your dreams,' I said.

'If you change your mind,' he said with a creepy smile, 'I'll be in room 27.'

'Good for you,' I said. 'I won't be.'

And he left also, to go and do whatever it was he did in room 27.

That appeared to be the end of the floor show for the night. I was pretty sure I'd had at least one conversation at cross purposes with somebody but wasn't certain if I was more worried that I had driven Jonathan Gold away or that I had received a warm and open invitation to join the Weasel for bedroom-based fun (bring your own drink). So that was that—it was off to my own lonely bed, which was not so much of a novelty for me as you might think.

There were only two really strange little incidents that occurred in the next sixty seconds.

First, passing the reception desk I saw the receptionist having a heated conversation with the chef. My French was just about up to it, and they were saying this:

RECEPTIONIST: Well, you should lock the [word not understood] things away then.

CHEF: How the [several words not understood] do you expect us to keep the kitchen locked when we have to use it to prepare food? It must have been one of the guests.

RECEPTIONIST: You think one of our guests is using it to slice a grapefruit maybe?

CHEF: Careful—it's that |words understood, but surely misheard?| English woman. Shut up for a moment.

'*Bon soir, Madame,*' said the Chef and Receptionist together, with smiles that did not seem totally genuine.

'*Bon soir, Messieurs,*' I replied.

I carried on very slowly indeed, but all I heard for my pains was:

CHEF: Come to the kitchen if you do not believe me.

RECEPTIONIST: How can I leave this desk unattended?

CHEF: Who will need you at this hour?

RECEPTIONIST: This is utterly pointless—but very well. I cannot be away more than five minutes.

Not much to go on there, as I think you will agree.

The second strange incident—bearing in mind my earlier conversations—was that I came across the fat Mr Davidov and the nice Mr Gold in an urgent whispered conversation. They stopped abruptly when I saw them and they too smiled at me in a tight-lipped sort of way.

'Good night, dear lady,' said Davidov with the lowest bow his waistline would permit.

The very nice Mr Gold just scowled at me, but eventually got out the words: 'Yes, goodnight, Miss Thirkettle.'

Their conversation did not seem to concern me at all but, even so, I did not stay and try to listen to it. Had I hidden round the next corner I might have learned a great deal and prevented multiple murders. But then again, maybe not. You can, in my experience, waste a lot of time casually eavesdropping on complete strangers. And I did have one of Apollinaire's chocolates waiting for me in my room.

Had I known what was to come, I would have sat in my room with a stop-watch, noting when all of the different noises occurred. As it was, the best I would be able to give the police in the morning was that I heard somebody entering the room next to mine—or possibly another nearby room—not long after I went to bed. Some minutes—or possibly hours—later I heard the door open and close again. At the same time, or perhaps very much later indeed, I thought I heard feet moving very rapidly and a bathroom tap ran for a long time. Then a muscular, dark haired man ripped my clothes off with his teeth while feeding me peach truffles. No, I think I must have dreamt that, because shortly after that I woke up to hear the dustcart outside, noisily loading hotel rubbish. The fact is that I usually sleep pretty soundly, so there isn't much point in asking me what happened overnight, as the police soon discovered. Still, these fragmentary memories gave me something to think about as the case unfolded.

I knew Ethelred would be up early and sitting in the restaurant half an hour before they started to serve breakfast, so he and I found ourselves alone when the croissants and coffee made their appearance. We were not the only ones up and doing, however. Mr Davidov was at the reception desk as I passed it. He too was giving the receptionist a hard time.

'You must,' he was saying, 'have given me the wrong envelope.'

'There was only one in the safe,' said the receptionist, not
I suspected for the first time that morning. His expression was
both annoyed and weary.

'But, I tell you, this envelope was empty when I opened it.'

'Then it must have been empty when you gave it to me,' said
the receptionist.

'Why would I give you an empty envelope?'

'How can I possibly know that?'

'But why would you put an empty envelope into the safe?'

'We put into the safe whatever we are given to put into the
safe. We do not check the contents. If a guest gave us an empty
envelope, we would put it in the safe, if that was what he wished
us to do. That is the service we provide.'

'You must remember that the envelope I gave it you clearly
had something inside it.'

'Do you think I remember every little detail of every little
thing that is handed to me?'

They glared at each other.

'Show me the safe,' demanded Davidov suddenly.

'I cannot show you the safe.'

'Show me the safe.'

'I cannot show you the safe.'

They sounded as though they were rehearsing some sort of
comedy double-act, and were being slow in reaching its punch-line.

'I demand that I am allowed to search the safe,' said Davidov,
thumping the counter.

'*Monsieur*, what *exactly* are you looking for?'

'That is none of your business.'

'Then I am unable to assist.'

'I insist that you assist.'

'You cannot insist that I assist.'

'I insist that I can.'

'You cannot insist that you can.'

'You cannot tell me what I can insist and what I cannot insist.'

'You cannot tell me what I can tell you.'

'I can tell you what you can tell me.'

They both paused thoughtfully at this point, and eyed each other up for a moment in silence. Davidov tried a new tack.

'The contents of my envelope are very valuable. If you refuse to help, then I must speak to the manager.'

'This is most irregular, Monsieur Davidov. But I shall speak to the manager myself. If he permits, I shall allow you to look in the safe, after breakfast. But there was only ever one white packet. You have it there.'

'Then you have allowed somebody else access to the safe. Somebody has taken my envelope and replaced it with this one.'

'Nobody has the combination except for me and the manager. You may rest assured of that.'

'I shall return after breakfast,' said Davidov. 'I have to check out of the hotel at nine o'clock. By that time, I insist that you will have found my envelope.'

I waved to Davidov as I passed but, in his distress, he did not even see me. He must have been very fond of his white envelope.

When I mentioned this to Ethelred he just nodded and chewed his croissant a bit. When the Davidov-receptionist incident reminded me that I had earlier caught Davidov and Gold in a cosy tête á tête, Ethelred was a little more interested.

'Impossible,' he said. 'Quite impossible.'

'Why?' I was curious to know, seeing that I had been there and Ethelred hadn't.

'You forget I have been staying here longer than you. Davidov is what is termed an oligarch.'

'Meaning?'

'Literally, a member of a small elite ruling a state in ancient Greece.'

'Thanks, Ethelred, but I meant in real life? How did he make his money exactly?'

'Davidov, as you would know if you read a newspaper or two, is a powerful Russian businessman with dubious but immensely valuable political connections. His base, to the extent he lives anywhere in particular, is Moscow, though he also spends a lot of time on his yachts. Nobody quite knows how he made his first billion, but he now owns an oil company, some mines, a nuclear reprocessing facility, a chemical works in India and various minor enterprises in Britain. He wants to buy an English football team, but there are plenty of people who want to block that because of Yacoubabad.'

'Is that Manchester United's wicket keeper?'

'No, it's the town in India that was poisoned by one of Davidov's factories—allegedly.'

Ah, yes, that one. Even I remembered the footage of that chemical leak and the newsreader saying in portentous tones: 'You may find some of the pictures in this report distressing'. I watched, but was glad that I wasn't the cameraman.

'That was bad,' I said. 'And how many...?'

'About seven hundred dead,' said Ethelred. 'There was an investigation of course and some surprise that it was not followed by Davidov's arrest and extradition to India.'

'How do you know all this?' I asked.

'It was in the all papers last year,' said Ethelred with a sigh. 'Don't you read anything except *The Bookseller*?'

'Yes, I read the literary reviews and *Hello! Magazine*,' I said. 'Frankly, when the best years of your working life are spent reading dross, the one thing you don't want to do in your spare time is read more dross.'

Ethelred said nothing.

'So, Davidov urgently needs to clean up his act then?' I said.

'If he wants to buy into the Premiership, then he will need to do more than a little public relations work. He will also need to dispel rumours of links to organised crime and the murder of a close business associate, who was found drifting in the Baltic. Of course, I'm sure that some people do go for a midnight swim under the ice in January.'

'So, you are saying that Davidov is staggeringly rich and unpleasant?'

'That is how some people would describe him, though it might be risky to do so in his hearing.'

'The thing that puzzles me,' I said, 'is what an oligarch is doing in a joint like this. Shouldn't he be somewhere where you can bath in champagne? Shouldn't he have half a dozen flunkies with Kalashnikovs to protect him?'

'This is the official hotel for the stamp fair. He has a genuine interest in stamps. He has also, he tells me, not forgotten his humble origins.'

A bit like my old man, then, who didn't forget his humble origins even though he eventually owned both vegetable stalls in the market. He didn't poison an entire town, of course, though it probably wasn't through want of trying.

'And Gold?' I asked.

'Jonathan Gold, conversely, is an environmental campaigner, with profound dislike of companies that treat the third world as a dumping ground for toxic waste. It is difficult to imagine him having a cosy tête á tête with Davidov about anything. In any case, I know for certain that they dislike each other intensely. The evening before you arrived I found them arguing in the sitting room. I thought they were about to murder each other.'

'But only in a figurative sense,' I added.

A waiter had crept up on us unobserved. He bent over and said very quietly. 'I am informing all of the guests that the police will need to speak to them.'

Well, I knew what that was about.

'You can tell them,' I said, 'that I never touched Mr Davidov's white envelope.'

The waiter looked puzzled. 'I do not know anything about that. The fact is that one of our guests has...died. Suddenly and unexpectedly. It will be quite impossible for you to leave the hotel until each of you has been questioned.'

'We have a train to catch,' I pointed out.

'Most of the guests are anxious to leave,' he said. 'Some very anxious indeed. There will be a lot of complaints, I think, but there is nothing I can do. The police have...some suspicions.'

I looked at Ethelred. He looked at me. The only thing that I was thinking that he was not thinking (I assume) was that I now had a chance to rectify my unfortunate misunderstanding with Jonathan Gold and set up a date for tonight if we were all still stuck here.

'Who has died?' asked Ethelred, apparently with no more than polite concern.

The waiter paused then said: '*Monsieur* Gold.'

'How?' I asked.

The waiter pulled a face. 'The unfortunate gentleman was stabbed. To death.'

So, that was the sort of day I was having. Stuck indefinitely in a hotel with peeling wallpaper, and the only fit guy in the whole place is the one they choose to murder. Bloody typical, isn't it?

CHAPTER 5

I always set my novels in England, preferably in Sussex.

A sense of place—preferably a location that you have established as your own from a literary viewpoint—is one of the keys to writing good modern detective fiction. Another is a detailed knowledge of police procedure. I have therefore tried to keep up to date with changes in practice, down to the minutiae of official record keeping. I have rarely been arrested in England, but should it happen in future, little would take me by surprise.

I neither know nor care, however, how the French police or the Italian police conduct a murder investigation, and at my age I have no plans to find out. Nothing in my experience as a crime writer had therefore prepared me for the questioning that I received that morning, in a small office, just off the main hotel reception.

The questions proved however to be routine and untaxing. Though my French was probably better than the police sergeant's English, I decided to let him do the hard work linguistically. Whenever there is the remotest chance of things getting tricky, you are always well-advised to stick to your own language.

So, I confirmed (in English) that I had arrived a few days before, from India, via Paris. I had, I explained, been travelling for some time to research my next book, but was about to return to London. I confirmed that I knew this part of France well, though I had not stayed in this hotel before, normally preferring a different establishment in town. I had been fortunate to obtain a room in a hotel full of stamp collectors.

'Fortunate?' asked the police sergeant.

'In the sense that I might otherwise have been sleeping in the street,' I said. 'Not in any other sense.'

'You do not like the stamps?'

'Until recently, I would have said that I was indifferent to stamps,' I said. 'But I have talked enough about them over the past three or four days to last me a lifetime.'

'So, it is that perhaps you dislike stamp collectors?' He found this interesting.

'Not sufficiently to murder one of them.' I smiled. He didn't.

'Perhaps somebody was not as tolerant as you,' he observed.

'You think that Mr Gold was killed simply because he was a philatelist? That seems a little harsh.'

The policeman shrugged. 'We think that too. In effect, we think he was not a philatelist. Is that so?'

'How would I know? How, for that matter, do you know?'

He gave me the policeman's stare. This was not something he really needed to tell me. But he did anyway. 'We have searched his room,' he said. 'There were no stamps. That is a little odd, no? To travel so very far and then to buy nothing?'

It struck me as a reasonable question, but I had no idea what the answer was. Collectors probably did sometimes go to stamp fairs without buying.

'Perhaps, like me, he just happened to be here?' I suggested.

'But you are here to…what do you say?…research your *roman*?'

'My book. Indeed.'

'*Monsieur* Gold on the contrary told the receptionist that he was here for the philatelic fair. Others saw him at the philatelic fair.'

'Perhaps he was selling something?'

'Yes, selling something, perhaps, though he did not register as a stamp dealer. We know in fact that he was a pharmacist by profession. Also that he had some interest in the environment. Of course, none of that prevents his being a collector of stamps. But we think that the fair was not his real reason for visiting France. Did he say anything that might have revealed what else he was doing?'

It was my turn to shrug, so I did. 'We spoke once or twice,' I said. 'We talked about the usual things that the English talk about when they meet each other overseas. On learning that I lived near Worthing, he asked me if I know an acquaintance of his who also lived near Worthing. Remarkably, I did not. Nor had he come across my great aunt who formerly lived in Finchley. I asked him if he had heard the cricket score. He had not. We wished each other a pleasant day.'

'That is the only conversation that you had with him?'

'No, I had others, but that was about as interesting as it got.'

'This is English irony?'

'Yes, this is English irony.'

'I see. Thank you.' For a moment I thought that the interview was at an end, then he added: 'What do you know about Jonathan Gold's relations with Grigory Davidov—I mean since the last few days?'

I had been wondering since breakfast how I would answer this inevitable question. I did not like Davidov, I had no views one way or the other about Jonathan Gold, and I had caught only part of their conversation. It was probably irrelevant in any case.

'I heard Mr Gold arguing with Mr Davidov,' I said.

'About what, please?'

'I can't be certain,' I said.

'But you *are* certain it was an argument? Then their voices must have been raised? Or perhaps one appeared to be about to strike the other?'

'Something like that.'

'But this could be important,' said the sergeant. He had ceased to take notes some time before, but now he reached for his pen. 'What precisely can you can remember, *Monsieur* Tressider?'

I closed my eyes and tried to picture the scene again. I had come across them in the sitting room—a small stuffy bolthole, painted wherever possible in shiny brown paint and provided with a number of uncomfortable, red plush armchairs and three or four incomplete chess sets. It seemed designed to dissuade guests from lingering, and to move them on to those parts of the hotel in which cash could be spent. It was an improbable location for anything except a conversation that was not to be overheard by other guests. I cannot remember now why I looked in, but the first thing I noticed was Gold with his fist raised, apparently about to punch Davidov on the nose. Davidov was laughing for some reason but, as I watched, the smile faded. It was as if he had just realised that a discussion that had started well enough was about to go badly wrong. 'That's not going to help get it back,' Davidov had smirked, but with an eye on Gold's fist all the same. 'You really don't understand what I could do to you, do you?' Gold had answered. It wasn't clear what he meant, but it could have been a reasonable point. Davidov was big, but my money would have been on Gold in a fair fight. I doubted, though, that Davidov had ever willingly entered into a fair fight. At that juncture my presence had been noticed, and Davidov had made a deep bow, leaving Gold shaking his fist rather improbably in mid air. Davidov looked at me standing on the threshold.

'You know that it's unlucky to stand there like that,' he said, with what seemed to be an attempt at humour. 'You should not hold a conversation standing in the doorway.'

'Another Russian superstition?' I asked.

'Yes,' he said.

'And is it unlucky for me or for you?'

'That is something that we would find out in due course,' he said. 'People who make bad luck for me, however, often have bad luck themselves.'

Davidov's tone was jocular, but Gold just stood there with his fists clenched by his side, looking at nobody in particular.

I had no wish to converse with Davidov from the doorway or otherwise, so I simply enquired whether there were any English newspapers in the hotel. Davidov immediately said he believed not. I departed to let them get on with whatever conversation they wished to get on with. But yes, now I came to think of it, that was precisely the exchange of words that I had overheard.

'You may be aware,' said the sergeant, 'that Mr Davidov had lost what he claimed was a valuable package, just before Gold's body was found. Could they have been arguing about that, for example?'

'No,' I said. 'I didn't know that. What sort of package?'

'The receptionist says that he was complaining that a white envelope had gone missing. He seemed very upset.'

It rang a bell. Had somebody mentioned it to me? If so, it had seemed less important at the time than it did now.

'Did he say what was in it?' I asked.

My question was pointedly ignored.

'Perhaps, sir, you could just tell me about the argument between Mr Davidov and *Monsieur* Gold? You say Mr Davidov had his fist raised?'

'Did I say that? I'm not so sure that's right.'

'So, no threat of violence?'

'I can't be sure.'

'But they were having an argument?'

'On second thoughts,' I said, 'describing it as an argument may be an exaggeration.'

'I thought you said...'

The sergeant looked at his notebook, but since he had not been taking notes at that point it told him nothing.

'So can you remember anything at all about their conversation?' the sergeant asked me, pen still poised.

I gave every appearance of considering his question. I wondered whether he would trade information about the white envelope for information about the argument, but I rather doubted that.

'That's about all I can tell you,' I replied.

The sergeant considered this in his turn and then shut his notebook with a dull thump. He screwed the top back on his pen and returned it to his pocket. He did not need to say how much of a disappointment I had been. 'Thank you, Mr Tressider,' he said. 'You have been more than helpful.'

'My pleasure,' I said.

CHAPTER 6

A general depression had fallen over the hotel. Every nook and cranny was occupied by people who wanted to be elsewhere. Whatever attraction either Chaubord or the hotel had for us before had evaporated the moment we were informed that we could not leave. Even Ethelred finally noticed that the hotel had a worryingly musty smell—something that I'd detected from Dover. In the sitting room the German family was trying to amuse itself with one of the incomplete jigsaws and not having much luck. In reception, a fair-haired bloke in a crumpled blue suit sat studying his map and chewing his biro. I hadn't seen him at dinner the previous evening, but I'd discovered him trying to check out after breakfast and protesting loudly in Birmingham-accented French when he was told that he would have to remain. Of all the unhappy bunnies in the hotel that morning he was, by just a whisker, the unhappiest.

I needed to get some air, but the only place to go was the hotel's small garden.

I found Ethelred already on the terrace there, drinking a coffee. He looked a little more pleased with himself than was good for him, but otherwise all was in order. Possibly he was just relieved that his interview with the police was over.

'How did it go?' I asked.

He was in the process of lifting his cup to his lips and now smiled at me across the frothy black liquid.

'It can't have gone *that* well,' I said. 'It's not as if you were ever a suspect. At the best, we're both free to leave before lunch.'

'I thought we might stay an extra night,' he said.

'OK, but why here?'

'Why not?'

'Well—number one,' I said, running through the obvious, as you often have to do with writers, 'it's a dump. It will probably be an empty dump by tonight if they let us go. Number two... actually, number one is plenty, Ethelred. It's a dump.' If I'd been planning a tryst with Jonathan Gold, I might have come up with some lame excuse for staying on. Who was Ethelred planning a tryst with?

Ethelred made some pretence of considering my arguments. 'No point in having the inconvenience of packing and unpacking,' he said. 'This is fine.'

'Fine? This is one of the worst hotels I have been in.'

'Anyway, I think I might make it a setting for my next novel,' he added, improbably.

'Then get your Moleskine notebook out and start scribbling. And do it fast. We're checking out at the very first opportunity.'

'I need,' said Ethelred, possibly telling the truth at last, 'at least to have a brief discussion with Grigory Davidov before we leave.'

'I thought you couldn't stand him? You described him as rich and unpleasant.'

'I said that's how some people would describe him.'

'So his friends just describe him as comfortably off and unpleasant?'

'Possibly. He's not the richest oligarch around by a long way. Even so, there's something important I need to ask him about.'

'What?' I asked.

'Oh, just something he told me that I wanted to follow up.'

'Well, you'd better move fast on that too,' I said, 'before the police arrest him. He has to be the prime suspect.'

'Why?'

'Because...duh...he and Jonathan Gold obviously did not like each other. Don't you think he's got to be the murderer?'

'The probability is that it was somebody from outside the hotel, and this business of holding us all here is totally unnecessary.'

'If Davidov wasn't the murderer then, at least, he and Gold were obviously cooking up something together.'

'Maybe.'

'So in that case,' I said, 'what if Mr Davidov knows who the murderer is?'

'I think that is very unlikely.'

'In one of your novels,' I said, 'the fact that somebody knew who the murderer was would mean that he was in imminent danger himself. He'd be the next one to snuff it.'

'Quite the contrary. That's not one of the clichés that I have ever used,' said Ethelred disdainfully.

Our conversation was interrupted by the French police sergeant, who had slipped out onto the terrace unnoticed by either of us. He bowed to me.

'Good morning, *Madame*,' he said.

'Are we free to go?' I asked.

'Unfortunately you will be here for a little longer,' he said apologetically. 'I regret to inform you that there has been a second death.'

He paused, waiting for the inevitable question.

'A second death?' asked Ethelred. Well, somebody had to or we'd be there all day.

'Mr Davidov has...died.'

'Meaning murdered?' I asked.

'A heart attack,' said the sergeant, though he did not sound convinced.

'That was bad luck,' said Ethelred, 'but, if that is the case, there should be no need to detain us.'

'Until we are certain of the cause of death, we must treat it as being suspicious,' said the sergeant.

'In other words, he's been murdered because he knew too much,' I said.

As a literary agent you get a feel for these things.

CHAPTER 7

If I had observed that the atmosphere had been muted during the morning, it was only because I had no idea how bad things would be by lunchtime. Maybe it was because the sun was shining and we couldn't go outside, other than into the rather sad little garden at the back of the hotel. Maybe it was because two of us had been murdered (heart attack? do me a favour) and the murderer was possibly still in our midst. For whatever reason, there was a collective depression that hung almost visibly over the dining room.

At our own little table, Ethelred was scowling and mono-syllabic. He seemed to have taken Grigory Davidov's death as a personal affront. At the next table the two German children were complaining (in German) that they were bored. I tried to make out some of what they were saying but, never having done even O level German, I could not understand a word. On the other hand anyone who has ever been around kids, and I do try hard not to be, would have immediately been able to recognise the whiney tone of the jaded infant. The fair-haired bloke in the crumpled suit, striped shirt and no tie had his map open in front of him, as though that would speed him on his way (strangely, it didn't). The two tweedy philatelists were silent and disgruntled.

The Weasel was absent, presumably in his lair.

'The police will want to question us all again,' I said.

'Especially you,' said Ethelred.

'Me? Since when was I any sort of suspect?'

'I didn't say you were, but your room is undeniably next to Davidov's.'

'Is it?'

I hadn't really noticed who was in which room, though I had the Weasel's room number. Mine was at the end of a corridor and so, thinking about it, adjoined Davidov's and no other. There was, I suddenly remembered, a connecting door in one wall of my room to permit speedy access between the two. My flesh crept, but only briefly, because the door had after all been firmly locked—I'd checked that. It might however explain why I had heard various noises as clearly as I had—because the door offered (slightly) less sound-proofing than a hotel wall. Davidov had certainly been restless last night—or somebody in his room had been.

I surveyed the dining room again while I mulled all of this over. It was full of lots of ordinary people with ordinary worries about missed connections and fractious offspring.

I had another dip into Ethelred's chocolate fondue (he was in no state to appreciate it) and then raised a question that had been troubling me. 'If it was one of the other hotel guests who murdered Davidov and Gold, which of us was it?'

Ethelred looked round the room without much interest.

'Exactly,' I said. 'There's nobody here who looks vaguely capable of one murder, let alone two.'

'But it could, as I have said, be somebody from outside the hotel,' said Ethelred.

'For the first murder, yes,' I said. 'But by the time Grigory Davidov died, the hotel had been sealed off. Nobody—guests or staff—could come or go.'

'So, a member of the hotel staff then. The chef would have had plenty of access to knives.'

That the chef might have taken a dislike to us all was not a happy thought. Still, I took another dip in Ethelred's chocolate fondue—some risks are worth taking.

'The chef? Do you think so?' I asked, licking my fingers.

'Not really. On the face of it is improbable that the hotel would contain two guests who had annoyed the staff enough that they should kill them both. One possibly, but not two. In the case of Jonathan Gold, most of the staff are in the clear anyway. As I think I mentioned, there were almost no staff on duty last night. The receptionist was the only one who was around the whole time, but he has apparently worked for the hotel for years and is not known to have any murderous tendencies. The hotel manager lives in, but as it happens was visiting friends in Tours; his car broke down and he and his wife were obliged to stay there until the following morning. All of the other staff—including the chef—live in the town somewhere and were absent at the critical time. When Davidov died, conversely, almost everyone was here. The odd thing about the second murder, though, is that it was committed in a hotel swarming with policemen. Not good timing, unless it was very necessary and you were very desperate. So, it's a bit of a puzzle. On the other hand, I'm only a crime writer. You'd be better asking the police what they think.'

'But, if you are saying that the murders are connected,' I said, 'then you are also saying it has to be one of the guests. But why should anyone murder two people as different and unrelated as Davidov and Gold?'

'Of course, we still don't know for certain that Davidov's death was murder,' said the practical Ethelred. 'The police said it could be a heart attack.'

'They would say that, wouldn't they?' I said. 'We need to find out what Gold and Davidov had in common.'

'As you say, very little,' said Ethelred.

'Mr Davidov had lost his valuable envelope,' I continued. 'The one that was in the safe. That has to be a clue, doesn't it?'

'Ah yes, the envelope,' said Ethelred, 'the police mentioned that.'

'No, I mentioned that,' I said. 'I saw Davidov arguing with the receptionist. I actually told you about it at breakfast, but you weren't listening as usual. Grigory Davidov had left an envelope in the hotel safe. When he checked the envelope this morning it was empty. He claimed whatever was in it had been stolen. The receptionist said that it must have always been empty.'

This made Ethelred very thoughtful.

'So you saw him? You saw the envelope? How large was it?' he asked.

'A4? No, more like A5, perhaps. Bigger than a normal letter anyway—maybe padded? I didn't see it up close. Davidov was in the process of handing it back to the receptionist. The receptionist didn't want it. What was amusing was that...'

'So, this valuable thing must have been quite small?' said Ethelred interrupting.

'Well, not enormous. I assumed it must be stamps—this being a stamp fair and so on. What else is small and valuable? Gemstones? Large denomination bank notes? Very very small works of art? A blackmail letter? Money makes sense—money to buy something that somebody here had...or...' My list trailed to a sad and anticlimactic close.

Ethelred said nothing.

'Maybe,' I continued, having had a comforting thought, 'Davidov and Gold were both, independently, trying to get hold of the same thing, and somebody else was trying to stop them both—even if it meant killing Davidov with half the French police force watching. That would be good in the sense that the rest of us, at least, have nothing at all to worry about, eh?'

I looked at Ethelred. For some reason, his face had gone quite white.

CHAPTER 8

I like to plan my novels in some detail.

I once met another crime writer who claimed to produce plans that were longer than the actual books. This seemed excessive, but perfectly possible. It's all about the small stuff. Though the reader should see nothing but unexpected twists and turns, as the writer you need a clear map showing the path through the maze, including many by-ways that neither you nor the readers will ever visit.

Take Ginger McVitie, for example, a personal favourite amongst my fictional villains. As the reader, you will gather he's been in and out of half the gaols in the country, and that's all you need to know. But, as the writer, I need to be familiar with exactly where and when and for what, otherwise I shall drop into my next novel the 'fact' that he was in Pentonville in 1992, and then some observant crime aficionado will be writing in to say that he was clearly there at the same time as Bruiser Beecham, so why didn't they recognise each other during the Buckford NatWest job in 1994? I sometimes have pages and pages of biographical notes for even the most minor characters. You may be able to breeze light-heartedly though horror stories, but you can't do crime superficially.

That's what makes it difficult for me to work with people who scarcely plan at all, as I was having to now. Of course, I had some idea what was required of me when I had arrived in France, but my instructions were (shall we say?) sketchy. It would have been helpful to have known who I was to meet up with and what it was that I was to collect. Little details of that sort. Davidov and Gold both looked, with hindsight, likely candidates as my 'contact', but neither had approached me and both were now inconveniently dead. If it had been either of them, I might as well go home as soon as we were released.

I had, as I had told the police, spoken only briefly to Gold, albeit on several occasions. With hindsight perhaps I should have had my suspicions about Gold's philatelic credentials from the start. In a hotel where stamps seemed the sole subject of conversation, he was the one of the few guests who never mentioned them.

Davidov, conversely, seemed to be a genuine enthusiast, only too willing to lecture me on his large and expensive collection. 'An entire room in my *Dacha* is devoted to stamps,' he said. 'It is my escape from the pressures of running so many successful businesses. I have many specimens dating to the time of the Czars. Of communism, I do not care to collect. But stamp collecting is a most egalitarian pastime, no? To collect classic cars (as I also do, by the way) takes money. To buy yachts costs money. But anyone can start a stamp collection with a few pennies, and anyone with a little knowledge will soon start to find bargains. I myself have found many bargains. Many.'

Then there was the weasely Mr Herbert Proctor. 'Call me Herbie,' he'd said when we first ran into each other, advancing a damp palm in my direction. 'What should I call you?' 'You call me 'Mr Tressider',' I had replied. I cannot say why I didn't like him. I have no idea at all whether he liked me. Probably not. But, though he looked as if he might have the capacity to bear grudges, he also appeared to lack the courage to do much about it. However frequently I snubbed him, he would bob up again, undeterred, with the same half-ingratiating, half-mocking smile. Though he had a knack of suddenly appearing in the chair next to mine, he gave no indication that he and I were supposed to be working together. I hoped we were not.

I initially wrote him off as just another stamp collector. What gave him away was that he talked about the same stamps over and over again, as if he had read a couple of articles before he left for France and was relying on those and those alone to see him through the next few days. It didn't bother me in the sense that one stamp was pretty much like another and I'd done exactly the same thing to cover my own tracks. He was actually one of the more interesting people at the stamp fair. It just happened that I didn't like him. Not a bit.

The nice family did not in any sense match my idea of what my contact would look like, though (as I was beginning to realise) that did not mean they were not the people I was supposed to meet up with. I chatted a bit to them in English and in their own language, but mainly in English. He was a diplomat and they were taking the opportunity for a short holiday in the country they had just been posted to. They were, as far as I could see, exactly who and what they claimed to be.

The fair-haired man was named Brown. He was in France on business—which was not in any way stamp-related. He was driving back to England and had stopped over at the hotel for one night. I had spoken to him only briefly before Elsie arrived. He was probably now regretting not pushing on to Caen that evening. He appeared to have pitched up totally by chance.

And the point was that my contact was to make himself or herself known to me during the course of the stamp fair. I was, for some reason, not to make the approach myself, even if I guessed who it was. Nobody had approached me however and nobody looked likely to.

What hadn't occurred to me, until Elsie kindly suggested it, was that there was any risk in this at all. Now it seemed to me that there might be quite a lot of risk. And I didn't even know what I was taking the risk for.

So, you could say, it was all a bit of a mess, even before Elsie had thoughtfully cancelled my credit cards.

I do hate it when people just give you part of the story. Don't you?

CHAPTER 9

There's not much you can do in a room without chocolate.

I'd been interviewed again by the police, which provided me with a little entertainment. Now I was sitting on my hotel bed, literally kicking my heels. I wondered whether to go and chat to the policeman outside. He was not, of course, guarding my door, but guarding the door to (the late and probably murdered) Mr Davidov's room to prevent anyone entering and tampering with the evidence.

I looked again at the connecting door and wondered how nervous I would have been if I had known Davidov was on the other side? Less nervous maybe than if it had been Herbie Proctor.

I wandered over to the door, turned the handle and gave it an experimental push. No, it was definitely locked. Then equally experimentally I tried my hotel door key in the lock and (what do you know?) the lock turned smoothly and it swung open to reveal...another door. So much for that then. Each room had, independently, its own connecting door operated by the same key as the door that led to the corridor outside. The keys to both rooms were thus needed to get them to interconnect, as and when interconnecting rooms were required.

I was shutting my own door again, when I noticed that the second, apparently closed, door moved slightly as I did so. Not only wasn't it locked, it wasn't even shut properly. Possibly

Davidov had been interested to see where his door went, or possibly the police had opened it speculatively when they were searching the room. Whoever it was, by kindly leaving the second door unlocked, they had just provided me with a way of enlivening an otherwise dull afternoon. With more than mild curiosity, I gave Davidov's door the lightest of touches. It swung open, silently and invitingly, and I stepped across the threshold.

I don't get to visit many crime scenes and my immediate reaction was that they were, after all, not that interesting. I found myself in a hotel room, very much like my own. Hanging on a hook on the outer door (still guarded on the far side by an unsuspecting policeman) was a standard hotel-issue dressing gown of cheap white towelling. The double bed was unmade and a large pair of pyjamas was strewn over the floor in a way that most mothers disapprove of. A capacious and probably very expensive suitcase was over by the wall. It was locked, but I knew that most people never change the original combination. I set the three little wheels to zero, zero, zero and it opened smoothly and discreetly to reveal its contents. There were shirts, some packets of what appeared to be prescription medicines, some improbably large pants, a tie, a couple of shiny, unread paperbacks in Russian—no clues there. I shut the case and re-fastened the catch.

On the dressing table, I found something worthy of my attention. There was a box of high-grade chocolates, with only one missing. Lots of yummy flavours—though, strangely, no peach truffles. This was odd, but in all other respects it looked a sound selection. I pictured Grigory Davidov going into Apollinaire to purchase this, his last ever box of chocolates. I pictured him choosing these chocolates that, tragically, he would never live to enjoy. I pictured him carrying them home, perhaps planning (as you do) the order in which he would eat them. I can't be certain, but I think a small tear may have run down my cheek at this point. I doubted that the police would bother to count chocolates, and I knew that the ghost of my former chocolate buddy would be looking down at me kindly. He would *not* want these chocolates to go to waste.

The next thing that I remember clearly is that I was sort of floating round the room with milk chocolate and creamy filling melting slowly in my mouth.

The chocolate concentrations in my body restored to safe levels, I returned to my investigations with a new energy and purpose. I checked the pockets of Davidov's jacket hanging in the wardrobe. There was a wallet in it with credit cards and quite a lot of cash. If he was happy to keep this much lying around, was it likely that it was cash in the envelope in the safe? Since the cash had no soft fondant centre, it was at no risk from me anyway. I replaced the wallet and closed the wardrobe door.

I had to admit that I wasn't coming up with much, and was obliged to reward myself with more chocolate just to keep going. The dressing gown was almost the last thing that I tried. What I found wasn't much, but it was very odd. In the left-hand pocket there were three things. A couple of Pound coins and, bizarrely, a receipt from a kosher restaurant in North London. Well, no reason why you shouldn't have a Jewish oligarch. I checked the date on the receipt and it was only a few days beforehand— that is to say Davidov had been in London immediately before coming to France. And paying cash for smoked salmon followed by Mehren Tzimmes with Knaidel.

There was a noise outside, reminding me that the police might also want their turn in the room at some stage. And I figured they would probably like some privacy when they did. I silently tiptoed back through the door, clutching a box with its two remaining chocolates. I pulled Davidov's door shut and then, very softly, closed my own and locked it.

It was at this point that I realised I was also still clutching the receipt and the coins. I might have gone back and returned them, but through the connecting doors (one locked, one not) came the very distinct sound of police activity in French. If I was going to take the receipt or the chocolates back, then it would have to be later. It was all evidence that they might need. On the other hand I did not wish to get arrested as an accessory of some sort while attempting to do my civic duty. I ate the last two chocolates while I wondered what to do.

I turned the coins over a couple of times as if they might tell me something, but they didn't. They were just regular pound coins bearing the Queen's head and, I now realised, my slightly sticky fingerprints. The receipt seemed to be for a meal for one and excluded service. Davidov had drunk a Diet Pepsi with the meal. He had not had a dessert, but had ordered an espresso. I still wasn't certain what I had found, but I was pretty sure it was important.

Still, it's annoying knowing only half the story.

I found Ethelred back on the garden terrace, surveying such view as there was, sipping another coffee.

He listened attentively to my account, which omitted any reference to orange creams or praline enrobed in bitter chocolate.

'There was no sign of the missing envelope, I suppose?' he said.

'None,' I replied. 'But surely Davidov had had that stolen?'

'So he claimed,' said Ethelred. 'I had hoped that was just a ruse.'

'Hoped?' I said.

Ethelred shrugged. 'I meant, I had wondered if it was a ruse...but obviously not,' he said. He had turned his attention to the receipt. 'I assume that it is your plan to let the police have this in due course?'

'I thought I might sneak it back tonight,' I said.

'That would be wise.'

'It's odd that Davidov would put this stuff in his dressing gown,' I said.

Ethelred shook his head. 'Don't forget that men don't usually carry handbags,' he said. 'All sorts of stuff ends up in your pockets. You empty your trouser pockets before you hang the trousers up. You have to transfer the stuff somewhere. A bedside table is good, but dressing gown pockets are often handy too.'

'But why,' I said, 'would Davidov pay a visit to London and seek out an obscure kosher restaurant for a fairly ordinary meal? What is...' I checked the bill again, '...Mehren Tzimmes with Knaidel, anyway?'

'Carrot pudding with dumplings,' said Ethelred knowledgably. It's the sort of strange stuff he knows. He's useful at pub quizzes. 'Very nice, I'm sure; but, as a clue, it's not much to go on.'

'Perhaps Davidov already knew Gold,' I said. 'Perhaps he had been over to London and had taken him to this restaurant.'

'Where only one of them decided to eat? It's bizarre, though perhaps only marginally less bizarre than an oligarch popping over from Moscow to enjoy a solitary dinner in Finchley.'

'Maybe they had separate bills,' I said.

'Maybe,' said Ethelred.

A hotel minion appeared for long enough for me to order a hot chocolate. While I waited for it to arrive, Ethelred and I sat in silence surveying the bedraggled winter garden. Even in summer it can't have looked much but now, with the grass overgrown and the token swimming pool hidden under its washed-out blue nylon cover, it looked melancholy and resentful. The last few roses had clearly had a suicide pact with the geraniums. Only the miserable, drooping laurels were genuinely content with their surroundings.

The garden must have developed into what it was through a series of random and entirely uncoordinated developments on the part of successive managers. One had evidently been a fan of concrete. Another had apparently tried to soften this with a row of fairy lights along the back wall—blatant Christmas decorations, but not this year's. The new summerhouse was a feeble attempt at the picturesque. The swimming pool was an unsubtle but inadequate ploy to gain a higher rating from the tourist authority; I wouldn't have been tempted, even at the height of summer.

A high brick wall separated this small earthly paradise from that of another hotel on one side and from a narrow lane on the other. On the side bordering the lane, a wooden gate offered, in happier times, an exit to the street and all chocolate shops beyond. On the remaining side, behind the hotel, damp water-meadows, full of flaccid weeds, stretched away towards the misty Loire.

It struck me that, even if the gate was locked, the wall was just climbable and I said so in passing to Ethelred.

'They have a policeman watching the garden, just in case you are thinking of making a break for it,' he said. He pointed towards the token summerhouse, where a chilly and disgruntled officer sat, rubbing his hands. I had not been thinking of making a break for it, but such a move had clearly been pre-empted.

'How much longer are they going to keep us here?' I muttered.

'Maybe not much longer,' said Ethelred. 'They seem to be half way through their second round of questioning.'

'Just so long as no other silly tosser gets murdered,' I observed.

'Hardly likely,' said Ethelred. 'Oh, I do have one piece of information for you, by the way—hot off the press. The police now know how Mr Davidov died.'

'How?' I asked.

'It wasn't very subtle,' said Ethelred. 'Somebody had put cyanide in his chocolates.'

CHAPTER 10

I have always found poison immensely convenient.

I am not the only writer to appreciate its merits. Agatha Christie was a great one for cyanide. In several of her books, she enjoys her first poisoning so much that she offers us a second before the end. I rarely poison more than one of my characters at a time, but I do poison them whenever the opportunity arises.

Poison has many advantages for the murderer. Unlike a gunshot, it is silent. Unlike a knife or axe, the murderer does not get covered with an inconvenient amount of the victim's blood. The fastidious killer does not need to take his hands to the victim's flesh, which is more or less essential for a strangling. Poison requires no physical strength and less courage than almost any other weapon. With a slow acting poison, the murderer can be far away before the victim has the first inkling that anything is amiss. This is often helpful. Of course, a succession of inconsiderate Acts of Parliament have made poisons more and more difficult to obtain, but since rat killer and anti-freeze are lethal enough in the right dose, this fact alone should not deter the aspiring poisoner.

Many of the best real life crimes are poisonings. George Orwell pointed out that of the eight most celebrated cases from the age he describes as 'our great period in murder' (1850-1925), no fewer than six were poisonings. More recently one of our most prolific killers used diamorphine to kill an estimated 250 victims—though, frankly, you could never get away with that number of deaths in fiction.

I have to confess to a weakness for cyanide myself. It is, other than for a faint smell of bitter almonds, not easily detected in food or drink. A 50 mg dose will cause death by anoxia within five minutes. Once you've taken it, there's not much going back. It's the one you choose when your suicide is not just a cry for help.

Arsenic takes longer, but is a good certain killer from multiple organ failure. Both As_2O_3 and As_2O_5 are colourless, odourless and readily soluble in water. Two of Orwell's golden age murderers (Seddon and Cotton) employed arsenic to good effect. In *Strong Poison* Dorothy Sayers adds it to an omelette. It's a reliable standby for the busy author.

Aconite is one of the older ones and has sometimes been called the Queen of Poisons. It is a white powder that dissolves in alcohol, which is fine other than for victims who are teetotallers. The consumer experiences a numbness and tingling in the mouth immediately after swallowing, followed by a parched sensation in the throat. The feeling spreads to the hands, feet and then to the whole body. Death is usually from a failure of the respiratory system after eight minutes to four hours. One fiftieth of a gram is sufficient to kill a real or fictitious person.

I reserve strychnine only for those I really dislike. It is not a nice poison. Shortly after taking it, the victim feels that they are going to suffocate, as indeed they are. Eventually. First the facial muscles start to contract and the face is pulled into a hideous grin called the Risus Sardonicus. Then other muscles start to contract causing violent and spasmodic contortions of the whole body.

Cruelly, in between each paroxysm, there is a short remission, during which the exhausted victim can believe briefly that the worst is over. But it isn't. With a livid face and clenched jaws, the victim dies of suffocation after two to three hours.

Occasionally it's good to go for one of the lesser-known poisons. Agatha Christie uses an eserine-based eye medicine in *Crooked House* and taxine in *A Pocket Full of Rye*. Dr Crippen selected hyoscine in his wife's case (but it didn't work, so he had to shoot her after all, which was a shame). It pays to keep people guessing.

Poisonings are not always deliberate. The Bradford Sweets Poisoning of 1858 is one of the more famous examples. William Hardaker (Humbug Billy as he was known) succeeded in poisoning two hundred of his customers with peppermint-and-arsenic humbugs. The supplier of Billy's humbugs was one James Neal. Neal had intended, he later said, to adulterate his sweets only with plaster of Paris—which was cheaper than sugar and not terribly harmful. He delegated its purchase however to his lodger, James Archer, who had only a vague idea of what he was after. The pharmacist who normally supplied Neal was sick and left *his* assistant to locate the 'daft', as it was known and package it up for Archer. Had he said clearly that the 'daft' was in the cellar next to the arsenic, then the assistant might have realised that he needed to be careful. Instead, James Archer came home proudly clutching twelve pounds of arsenic—enough to kill roughly two thousand people. This Neal used along with forty pounds of sugar, four pounds of gum and a dash of peppermint essence to produce the next batch of sweets. Billy noticed that the batch looked a bit different and cannily negotiated a discount. In the end it was surprising that only twenty of his customers died.

Personally, if it were me being murdered, I'd go for a very large dose of diamorphine. Interestingly, Harold Shipman, after a successful career poisoning others, chose to hang himself in Wakefield Prison. But there is, as they say, no accounting for taste.

Elsie is not somebody who was designed for speed, but one moment she was sitting next to me on the terrace and the next she was being violently sick in the bushes. It was a pale and repentant literary agent who resumed her place on the chair beside me. I tried to keep a straight face as she confessed how she had disposed of one key piece of evidence.

'Had you paused long enough to ask me, I might have been able to reassure you,' I said. 'Grigory Davidov must have died almost instantly, after apparently consuming a single chocolate. You ate eleven half an hour ago. What does that suggest to you?'

'The others were just regular chocolate? Hold the cyanide?'

'That is a reasonable assumption. Had any of the truffles contained even a fraction of the poison in the one eaten by Davidov, you would be very sick indeed by now—and probably dead—rather than merely queasy.'

'But Davidov had eaten only one from the box. Wasn't it a bit of a coincidence that he ate the only poisoned one?'

'I think that his chocolate must have been poisoned by somebody who knew him well—somebody who knew exactly which one he would choose first.'

Elsie frowned.

'There was no peach truffle left in the box,' she said with a clear sense of grievance.

'A poisoned peach truffle it was then,' I said. 'A lethal peach truffle precisely and knowledgably targeted by somebody who had access to poisons.'

'Well, you might have told me before,' she muttered.

'I didn't know before, and I certainly had no way of predicting that you would start eating key pieces of evidence so shortly after lunch.'

'I ought to sue the French police, leaving dangerous chocolate lying around like that.'

'To be fair, they also had no idea until a few minutes ago that Davidov had been poisoned—let alone that it was in the chocolate. They had moreover locked the door and placed a twenty-four hour guard on it to prevent anyone doing what you did. But I agree that in all other respects they were most negligent. Would you like to know, however, what else I have discovered?'

Elsie did, but was prepared to admit it only by way of a slight moderation of her scowl.

'I was able to find out a little more about Jonathan Gold's murder. The sergeant is quite a devotee of crime fiction and had actually read one or two of my books in the *Editions Belfond* translations. He became quite chatty after a while and was willing to help me in my research for the next Fairfax case.'

'I thought you weren't going to write any more Fairfaxes?'

'I'm not, but he doesn't know that. What he told me was interesting. It would seem that Gold let his assailant in—there was no sign of the door or window being forced. It was late enough that he had already got changed for bed, though you implied he may have opted for an early night anyway.'

'Yes,' she said, avoiding my gaze. 'He must have been extremely tired.'

'He was in his pyjamas in any case. His blood-stained dressing gown appeared to be thrown over him—possibly he was holding it when he fell or perhaps it had been loosely draped over his shoulders. There was no hole corresponding to the knife wound in the dressing gown anyway. The police theory is that he was in bed and got up to answer a knock at the door. He picked up the dressing gown as he did so, but never had time to put it on. There was no sign of any struggle—nothing broken, no furniture over-turned— again suggesting that whoever entered the room was able to do so without arousing suspicion or alarm. Jonathan Gold must have been caught completely off-guard. We have to assume that it was somebody he knew and that it was all over very quickly. The rooms on both sides of Jonathan Gold's happened to be empty. Nobody seems to have heard anything. It was a single stab wound from a sharp, broad-bladed knife, delivered with some strength. There was no sign of the murder weapon, but the killer would have had several hours to dispose of it before the body was found.'

'The dustmen woke me up,' said Elsie thoughtfully. 'If it had just been dropped in with the kitchen waste, it could be under several feet of landfill by now.'

'Or the river is very close by,' I added. 'I have no doubt the police will have thought of both possibilities.'

'I...' said Elsie, and then stopped in her tracks. We were no longer alone on the terrace. Herbert ('call me Herbie') Proctor had joined us.

Proctor made less noise as he moved around than almost anyone I have ever met. His size seven feet must have been encased in the softest soled shoes around. He was also of a height not to attract attention. His five foot five (or six) frame did not make him conspicuous in the hotel bar or elsewhere. His clothes seemed chosen for their lack of identifiable style or character— today it was stone coloured moleskin trousers, a cream shirt and a slightly faded, green, zipped fleece. I wondered how long he had been standing there before we noticed him.

'What do they charge for a coffee out here?' he asked. 'I'm not paying extra just to drink it in the freezing cold.'

'It's free,' I said, 'like the lunch. So long as we are obliged to stay here, the hotel has offered not to charge.'

'Lunch was *free*?' muttered Proctor. I remembered that he had been absent from the dining room. 'Well, somebody might have told me. Is dinner free too?'

'I assume so,' I said. 'If we're all still here.'

'I'll eat double at dinner, then,' he said, with a sort of grim determination. He deposited himself, uninvited, in a chair at our table. 'Well, what were you two young people talking about?'

'About the death of two of the hotel guests,' I said. 'Like everyone else here, probably.'

'And what have the police got to say about that?' he asked.

'They have revealed very little,' I replied cautiously. 'To me at least.'

'They ought to let us all go,' said Proctor. 'It's obviously none of the guests who did it.'

'Why are you so sure?' I asked.

'Well, if it is, then it makes even less sense keeping us all cooped up here so the murderer can pick us off one by one. But it's much more likely that it's somebody from outside. Or one of the staff.'

'Do you know something that we don't?' I asked.

Proctor smiled and tapped his nose. 'You'd be surprised what Herbie Proctor finds out,' he said. 'Anyway, I doubt any of these stamp collectors would be up to murder. Pathetic bunch.' He raised an eyebrow, asking us to share this low estimation of the hotel guests.

'Pathetic bunch? You mean your fellow philatelists?' I enquired.

He look blank and then said: 'Oh, right, yeah.'

'You think that stamp collecting is a rather sad pastime, perhaps?'

'No, not at all,' said Proctor, with a gleam in his eye. 'At least we stamp collectors get out and meet people—not like being a crime writer, scribbling away on your own.' He grinned at me. 'There—you didn't think I knew you were an author, did you? People always underestimate me at their cost. Well, I'll tell you, not a lot escapes Herbie's attention. Only met you a day or two ago, but I bet I could tell you plenty about yourself. Actually, I'm a bit of a fan of yours—I like the Buckford novels—though I always think your Sergeant Fairfax is a bit hard on private detectives.'

'Fairfax believes that crime is the business of the police and nobody else. So do I, as it happens. And you're a bit off target as far as crime writers are concerned—we are actually quite a sociable bunch.'

Proctor was unimpressed. He seemed to have a fairly low opinion of humanity generally and was not prepared to be surprised or to give crime writers the benefit of the doubt on my say-so alone.

'You haven't thought of writing a novel about a private eye, then, Ethelred?' he continued.

'No,' I said.

'It's not just the police who can pick up clues, Ethelred.'

'Yes, Mr Proctor, I'm afraid that it is,' I said. 'That is precisely how it works in real life. A private investigator may be helpful in a divorce case or industrial espionage, but they wouldn't have much to teach the police about murder.'

Proctor looked at me, clearly nettled. 'You think so? Well, perhaps I already know just a bit more about Gold's and Davidov's murders than the police do.'

'So what do you know?' asked Elsie.

Proctor looked from me to Elsie, then back to me. He smiled and tapped the side of his nose again. 'That, boys and girls, would be telling. That really would be telling. Now, where do I get some of that lovely free coffee?'

I glanced over towards the door, where I had thought I noticed somebody a moment before. But if there had been a waiter there, he had gone now.

'Try reception,' I said. 'They'll tell you.'

He sniffed. 'Might just do that,' he said. 'See you both later.' And he silently slipped through the terrace door and was gone.

'Well,' said Elsie, 'he can spot a writer at thirty paces all right.'

'Hardly a difficult trick,' I said. 'He would have only had to overhear a few words between us at dinner or over breakfast. And if he checked my name in the hotel register a Google search would give him all the information he needed—there are all sorts of places that could have told him which names I write under. Five minutes research would have been enough.'

Elsie raised an eyebrow when I mentioned 'Google'. One of her more pathetic running jokes is that I am still trying to get to grips with nineteenth century technology, let alone the twenty-first.

'Still, he must have been interested enough in you to run the search,' said Elsie, thoughtfully. 'What does he do—other than pretend to collect stamps? Was he trying to tell us he was a private eye?'

'I didn't ask him,' I said. 'Nor do I plan to.'

'Do you think he really does know anything we don't?' asked Elsie. 'If so, I wonder who else he's told, and whether that was wise?'

'You have a very vivid imagination,' I said.

It was about an hour later that the police sergeant found me in the sitting room.

'I am afraid that you will all have to stay until at least tomorrow morning,' he said. 'There seems to have been another attempted murder.'

'Another one?'

'A physician has been called for Mr Proctor. He too has been poisoned.'

CHAPTER 11

It was a pensive group of guests who gathered for tea in the echoing, baronial dining room. Though the hotel had gone to town in providing appealing sandwiches and yummy gateaux, few of us seemed to have much appetite. Possibly it was the weather, or possibly it was that two guests had recently been poisoned, one fatally. People picked at their food, pausing after each mouthful to see what would happen. Nobody was competing to be the first to try the nice cakes. We all checked what the others were eating and then watched them with more than casual interest.

I cut myself a modest second helping of Black Forest gateau, jiggled it around so that it almost fitted onto the plate, and rejoined Ethelred at our table.

The German family decided it had had enough and quit, the father nodding to Ethelred as they left.

'You'd have thought Germans would have been keener on Black Forest gateau,' I said. 'It's one of their better inventions, after all.'

Ethelred looked blank.

'The German family,' I repeated.

'They're not German,' said Ethelred. 'They're Danish. He works at the Danish Embassy in Paris.'

'Danish?'

'I was talking to the father. They're from Nykøbing.'

'Nykøbing? That rings a bell. Wasn't that where those rare stamps turned up?'

'Possibly,' said Ethelred.

'Yes, that's it,' I said, through a mouthful of chocolate crumbs. 'It was in a flea market in Nykøbing. How big is Nykøbing?'

'Pretty small,' said Ethelred. (Remember what I said about pub quizzes?) 'Why?'

'Well, that makes it a pretty big coincidence, doesn't it?'

'There were lots of stories in the newspaper. Some were about stamps, some were not. These people had to come from somewhere. Wasn't there also one about a gem robbery in London? Does that make you a suspect because you live in Hampstead?'

'London is a bit bigger than Nykøbing,' I pointed out.

'I'm not sure you've got the right place anyway,' he said.

'No, I'm sure it was Nykøbing—I remember the funny little line through the O.'

'Possibly, but you have to remember that...'

'What,' I said, 'if they had these puce things and were planning to sell them here before their ownership could be challenged in the courts? Or what if they were the original owners and had discovered...'

'What you have to remember...' said Ethelred interrupting me.

'But,' I said, re-interrupting Ethelred, 'you have to admit that it's possible.'

'Even if what you said were true—and it's unlikely for reasons that I have been trying to explain and that I won't bore you with now—but even if what you said were true, it doesn't explain two murders and an attempted poisoning.'

'But the stamps were really valuable.'

'Less valuable now there are three of them,' said Ethelred, showing he had been paying some attention when I first told him about it.

'But still valuable-*ish*,' I persisted. I tried to un-delete stuff from my memory. Wasn't a figure of a million dollars each quoted somewhere? I put this to Ethelred.

'Granted,' he said wearily. He looked like a man who had already had as many conversations about stamps as he was ever going to need.

'What,' I said, 'if they were going to sell them to Davidov? He's the sort who would have bought dodgy stamps with disputed owner-ship. He likes czarist stuff. Didn't the Czar rule Denmark once?'

'That was Finland.'

'Was it? OK, so what if he had the stamps in that envelope?'

'So who murdered him? Not the nice Danish family.'

'The original owner, maybe.'

'Who must have also presumably have been Danish, and who is clearly not here.'

I saw the logic of this. But surely a stamp fair like this, with loads of collectors milling around, was exactly where you would try to flog a valuable stamp of possibly disputed ownership? And this would have been one of the first stamp fairs to take place after the stamps had changed hands.

'No,' said Ethelred. 'Whoever has the stamps now could probably argue they had good title to them, even if they know they had been sold to them unintentionally. They wouldn't try to flog them cheaply and illicitly. They would be better off going to court if they had to and then selling the stamps in an auction. Nothing this big has come onto the market for some time—there's no knowing what a pair would fetch.'

'How much roughly?' I asked.

Ethelred sighed.

'The Swedish Treskilling yellow of 1855,' he said, 'last sold for a bit under three million Swiss Francs. That's the sort of price a unique specimen commands. The one-cent British Guiana black on magenta cost a million dollars—but that was back in 1980. Oddly neither stamp is in what you could describe as great shape. There's a story, by the way, that may be vaguely relevant to this case. A second British Guiana one-cent magenta surfaced in the 1920s. Arthur Hind, the owner of the first one, is said to have bought it and then to have used it to light his cigar. That way he preserved the value of his investment. Unique examples are the thing to have. Stamps like the Hawaiian Missionaries 2 cent—of which there are over a dozen—don't make more than a fraction of that sort of price. Potentially the single Danish ten kroner puce, so long as it was the only known specimen, was the most valuable of the lot. Ten kroner was a vast amount to pay for a stamp. It was probably intended for paying stamp duty rather than for postage—which is why it doesn't always appear in the standard lists of valuable postage stamps. But even if there are now three of them, then whoever has the two from Nykøbing is still onto a good thing.'

'Ethelred, I just asked *roughly* what it was worth.'

'All you need to know is this,' Ethelred said. 'Somebody might have all sorts of motives for wanting to get hold of the Danish stamps. But I don't think anyone would try to unload them here. And I don't think anyone would kill for them.'

'So what was in Davidov's envelope then?' I asked.

Ethelred opened his mouth as if to answer, then shut it again and just looked at me.

'How would I know that?' he eventually said.

It was almost dark out on the terrace, but I wanted to take one last look at the landscape before the light faded. I noted the line of the wall, the location of the policeman (flapping his arms to keep himself warm). I noted where the garden furniture was stacked up. I mentally measured the distance to the toilets in the hotel reception. Yes, this was, quite literally, for once, going to be a piece of piss. Everything depended on the chocolate shop staying open until six.

I was about to retrace my steps to a warmer place, when Mr Brown emerged onto the terrace and also started to survey the wall. I had not really had a chance to talk to him and it seemed a good chance for me to extract a few nuggets of information, if he had any to reveal. I therefore engaged him in a bit of intellectual conversation.

'It's brass monkey's right enough,' was my opening gambit.

'Sorry? Yes, I hadn't realised the Loire Valley could be this cold in December.' That seemed to be all the conversation he had for the moment. He bit a nail or two and looked at the wall, then at the policeman, then at the wall.

'Even if you make a break for it,' I said, 'they'll stop you at Caen. We're all suspects.'

'I know,' he said. So we were thinking along similar lines then, though he wasn't envisaging doing it in a Versace skirt and high heels or stopping off to buy chocolate truffles *en route*.

'You weren't planning on a long stay?' I enquired.

'I wasn't planning on any stay at all. I'd driven up from Bordeaux. I was getting a bit tired so thought I'd rest up in Chaubord and make an early start this morning. I really needed to be in England round about now. If I'm delayed any longer it will be a disaster. I keep checking the map to see if I can shave half an hour off the journey, but in the end I'm going to miss the conference I was supposed to be at tomorrow.'

'Oh right,' I said. Then as an afterthought I added: 'What sort of conference?'

'Pharmaceuticals,' he said.

'As in dangerous drugs?' I asked

'Most drugs are dangerous if misused,' he said. 'We like to think they all have a beneficial effect if properly prescribed.'

I studied him. He was carrying the odd surplus pound, but looked strong enough to carry out an efficient stabbing. He potentially had access to a wide range of poisons. He might well be carrying some with him. It would be interesting to know what he had stashed away. Time to lob in a few trick questions, I reckoned.

'I've got a bit of a headache—you wouldn't have anything for it I suppose?'

He gave a laugh. 'Sorry—I'm afraid I don't usually carry samples on business trips,' he said. 'I'm sure reception could find you some paracetamol.'

'Maybe something a bit stronger than paracetamol?' I said. 'Know what I mean?'

He looked at me oddly. 'No,' he repeated. 'No drugs of any sort. The police have been through my bags and pretty well taken the car apart. If I had any illegal substances on me, I can assure you I would have been under arrest long ago. So, no—I have no drugs for sale or otherwise. You'll have to wait until we get out of here for…whatever it is you want.'

Fine. He's got me down as a smack-head.

'Did you know either of the two murder victims?' I asked.

'How could I have done? The young guy was killed the night I arrived and Mr Denisov, or whatever he was called, died this morning. I hardly had a chance to speak to either of them.'

'No interest in stamps?'

'Strangely, yes, I have. I've collected them since I was five. But the stamp fair was pretty much over by the time I arrived.'

I switched the subject to the ten kroner puce but he just looked blank. 'I haven't had much time to look at the papers,' he said.

It seemed that it was going to be a fairly dull and uneventful evening.

Then I looked over Brown's shoulder and saw, coming through the door, Herbie Proctor's ghost.

CHAPTER 12

Men and women choose very different ways of getting themselves murdered. I will not pretend that my novels precisely reflect Home Office statistics for crime in England and Wales, but anyone embarking on a long string of fictitious killings should at least know something about the relative probabilities.

First, men are far more likely to get murdered than women. Anyone aiming for realism needs roughly twice as many male victims as female.

Women tend to be murdered by their partner or ex-partner. A justice system that automatically convicted the husband would get it right more than a third of the time. By far the majority of women who are murdered are killed by somebody who knows them well—if not by a husband, then by a devoted son or daughter. Often they are strangled.

Men, on the other hand, get out more and are likely—increasingly likely—to be killed by a stranger. Home is relatively safe for men. Wives, for some reason, murder husbands much less frequently than husbands murder wives. Less than ten percent of murdered males meet their death at the hands of an enraged spouse, though 'nagged to death' does not for some reason seem to be a Home Office category.

Men are most likely to meet their deaths at the pointy end of some sharp instrument—stabbings of one sort or another account for around a third of male murders. Stabbing leads however by only a short head from death by fist or boot.

In the UK it is relatively rare for either men or women to be shot, though in the United States it is of course routine, seventy percent of murders being committed with firearms in accordance with the Second Amendment. The right of the people to keep and bear arms ensures that nobody needs to mess around with less efficient methods.

Poisoning, which as I say is one of my personal favourites, accounts for a surprisingly small number of real life murders—just four or five percent, except in bumper years such as 2002/3, when Harold Shipman's victims skewed the figures just a tad.

Drownings, which you would imagine would figure reasonably highly, typically make up less than one percent. If you want to join a really exclusive club, however, then my advice is to get blown up. Murders by explosion are still fairly rare.

The age of murder victims follows a sinuous curve, with one peak between 16 and 30 years old. It falls for the over thirties and then again for the over fifties. The other peak is not, oddly, the very old, mugged by teenage tearaways for their pension books. The most dangerous year of your life, when you face the greatest risk of murder, is your first. If you're old enough to read this, then the good news is: the risky bit is already over.

I am not sure that the Home Office produces statistics for fictional murder. If it did, then a very different pattern would probably emerge. By far the most common way of dying in an Agatha Christie novel, for example, is poisoning, beginning with the *Mysterious Affair at Styles* in 1920 and ending with *Poirot's Last Case* in 1975. Christie's murderers also seem to be able to get their hands on guns fairly easily. A number of people are pushed abruptly from high places (not a Home Office category). Pretty well nobody gets a good kicking in a dark alley for no reason other than they looked at somebody the wrong way. Nobody gets knifed just because they suggested somebody else might like to pick up the sweet paper they had just dropped. People are killed deliberately for sound, practical reasons. It's what we mean by the Golden Age of Crime.

I don't know that modern crime writers are much more accurate. Victims die ingeniously and gruesomely, but there is usually still too much planning, too much *intent*. Most real murders are pointless, accidental, regretted within moments. Christie, it is said, used to write the first draft of her novels as far as the last chapter, then pause and consider who was the least likely murderer before going back and rewriting the book so he or she was the one who did it. It's a good literary anecdote, but I think she was pulling somebody's leg, frankly. Still she was right about one thing. Murderers include the most unlikely people. You'd never spot one in the street. Or in a hotel.

CHAPTER 13

'Y ou look,' said the sad remains of Herbert Proctor, 'as if you had both seen a ghost.'

He dumped himself down in a vacant chair in between Brown and me. Since he landed with a thump rather than a spectral breeze, we assumed he was less dead than he had immediately appeared. 'I suppose there's no sodding free coffee around?' he added dispelling the last trace of otherworldliness.

'I take it you know you look like death,' I said. His face was white and his eyes were hollow. He could have got a job as a corpse on any police drama he'd wanted. Any one at all.

'Look like death? And feel it,' he said. 'Bloody doctors.'

'What happened?' I asked.

He looked a little sheepish and then said: 'I got a really bad pain in the gut—honestly, really bad. So I said to the receptionist—oi, you, Pierre, I think they've poisoned me too; you'd better get me out of here sharpish and into hospital. Just so they can keep an eye on me.'

'And did they?'

'Yes. In an ambulance with all the lights flashing. They kept me under armed guard the whole time I was there. You'd have thought I was pretending to have gut ache so I could do a runner.'

'And you weren't?'

'They never gave me the chance, did they?'

'Even so, it doesn't sound that bad.'

'They only pumped my stomach, didn't they?'

'Not nice?'

'Try it sometime yourself and then give me your opinion.'

'No thanks,' I said.

'No flipping lunch, then they pump out what little there was in the first place.'

I told him there might still be free food in the dining room (though it was a bit of a long shot at this stage) and he sloped off still muttering imprecations against the French medical profession.

'What do you reckon?' asked Brown.

'As escape plans go,' I said, 'Herbie's was crap. He deserved to have his stomach pumped. For me it's over the wall or nothing.'

'You'd never get away with it,' said Brown.

'Watch and learn,' I said.

The wintry sun was low in the sky, casting elongated shadows over the concrete. Soon it would be dark. I headed for the bar and returned clutching the large glass of Jenlain Blonde that formed an essential part of the plan.

Actually Brown had long since got cold and bored and had already cleared off to the sitting room when I finally made my break. I had in fact needed to deliver three foaming and completely complimentary beers to the policeman on duty before he started to look uncomfortable and made a quick run for the *toilette* behind reception. I reckoned that gave me about a minute and a half.

I deftly fetched a white plastic garden chair from the heap and then shoved it hard against the wall. That provided just enough height for me to scramble up on top for a brief and exhilarating moment. It was not exactly comfortable perched there and the drop down to the street looked bigger than I had anticipated. But my cause was a noble one and I made a better landing than I hoped, bearing in mind I was not wearing sensible shoes and that my skirt had shrunk a bit at the dry-cleaners. I checked my watch—just time to get to Apollinaire before it closed.

The shop assistant was very sympathetic, and stayed open a few extra minutes while I selected enough truffles to fill their largest box. It is always a pleasure to watch a true artist at work. In front of the plain black dress and severe starched apron, her latex-gloved hands moved rapidly, selecting, transferring and always judging to a millimetre where each precious item should go. Once the last corner was occupied, she carefully closed the box, sealed it with a small red label and tied a gold ribbon around it. I handed her mere money in exchange.

As I left the shop I realised this was as far as my plan went. I had always been aware I would need to get *back* into the hotel, but had not given much thought to what came after buying chocolate, and perhaps eating the first two or three, reasoning that it would all sort itself out somehow. As I approached the garden wall, however, I realised that climbing in was going to be a lot more interesting than climbing out. To begin with, I had no step on the outer side, nor had I any way of knowing when the policeman's attention would be diverted. Possibly the best tactic was to go back to the main street and to breeze in through the neon-lit front door as if I had every right to be wandering the streets. I'm quite good at brazening things out when all else fails. It's a gift I have.

While I was pondering the options, I noticed something of more than passing interest. Mr Brown and I were not the only ones with escape plans. A small, shadowy figure was scrambling, with slightly greater agility than I had displayed myself, over the wall. The figure paused for a moment and then jumped, landing softly and cat-like in the shadows at the foot of the wall. It straightened itself to its unimpressive full height, revealing itself to be a weasely individual of familiar mien. Herbie, in spite of a very empty stomach, was having a second attempt at escape. It seemed he needed very badly to be somewhere else.

I watched him scuttle along the wall and then, as he reached the lights of the main street, slacken his pace to a more normal walk, before heading off in the direction of the railway station. Naturally, I followed. At first he seemed to be checking from time to time whether he was being tailed, but once clear of the hotel he gained confidence and he did not look back until just before he reached the station entrance.

I had expected him to head straight for the ticket *guichet* and buy a *billet simple* to somewhere as distant from Chaubord as he currently needed to be, but he just sailed on past it and towards the left luggage office. This was a curious escape plan. I tried to get close enough to see what he was doing, but SNCF had put disappointingly little cover around the station behind which an observer might stand and remain unobserved. Herbie was out of sight for a few minutes, but I had the only exit covered, so he at least could not go back into town without my knowing all about it.

If I was to tail him back to the hotel there was a further procedural difficulty. I was currently (with respect to the town centre) ahead of rather than behind him. He was obviously going to have to walk past me at some point in order to get us back in the right configuration of follower and followee. I therefore managed to back-track and conceal myself and my chocolates in an unlit bus shelter long enough to watch him start the return journey and to notice that he held what seemed to be a small silvery left luggage key on one hand. He looked pretty pleased with himself but (without cooperation from SNCF that I wasn't expecting to get) I didn't know exactly why.

On the return leg he was even less cautious than before, though I hung back and made maximum use of any bits of wall, tree, shadow and so on. He still appeared to have the key clutched in his hand as he turned the corner by the hotel for the climb back into the garden. For about sixty seconds he was out of sight in the side street, as I scuttled from my cover behind a billboard. It may be that at this stage I became over-confident in my sleuthing ability, because coming quickly round the corner myself, expecting to see his feet vanishing over the wall, I cannoned straight into him. He was standing back from the wall, possibly trying to resolve the same problem that I had noted myself—that is to say how to get back in without being arrested for getting out.

'Well, well,' he said, gulping audibly. 'Out on a little nocturnal ramble, are we?'

'Much the same as you,' I said. 'Just a little trip to the chocolate shop.'

'Not just to the chocolate shop. Did you think I didn't know you were following me?' he asked patronisingly.

'You didn't look round,' I said. 'Not once all the way back from the station.'

'I don't have to,' he said, tapping his nose. 'Especially when you seem happy to confirm that's what you did.'

'Then I hope you had a profitable outing,' I said.

'Profitable enough,' he replied.

I looked to see exactly what sort of key he had in his hand, but it was gone.

'You look puzzled, Elsie,' he said. 'Lost something?'

Then it struck me—if he had something he really wanted to conceal, the best thing would be to swallow the key and have no incriminating evidence at all about his person when he went back over the wall.

'No,' I said. 'I haven't lost anything. I wondered if you had?'

'Not me,' he said. His Adam's apple jumped as he gave another quick swallow.

'Sure?' I said.

'Sure,' he said.

'Then the only puzzle,' I said, turning to the immediate predicament, 'is how we get back in. The wall's pretty high and there's a policeman inconveniently positioned on the other side. One or both of us is going to get caught.'

Herbie looked me up and down and then said: 'I think I know how it can be done. I'll take a quick peek over the top—I'm a bit taller than you are, see? Then, as soon as the coast is clear, I'll give you a leg up. Once you're in and the policeman is looking elsewhere, you can pass the chair over the wall to me and I'll climb up.'

Waiting until the policeman would fail to notice me wandering around in the twilight rearranging the garden furniture struck me as a weakness in the scheme, nor was I convinced that Herbie was quite as tall as he thought he was. But it seemed a good plan in the sense that it got me in. That it didn't get both of us in was not my problem, and if Herbie didn't realise that I was getting the better of this particular deal, then *tant pis*.

After jumping up a couple of times and peering over the wall, Herbie announced in a stage whisper that we had our chance. I quickly placed a foot in his hand and he expertly hauled me up and onto the top of the wall. I jumped into the darkness, taking care to have a firm grip on the precious box. The good news was that my landing was softer than expected.

The policeman that I found underneath me however, his face now pressed into the soft but chilly flowerbed, was not what you might describe as best pleased.

I suppose I could have come up with any number of perfectly good reasons for my jumping from the top of the garden wall onto a guardian of the law on a fine winter evening, but none that I could think of seemed even remotely convincing at the time. I smiled sweetly, but the policeman did not seem keen to pass it off as a schoolgirl-ish prank as I hoped he might.

'Ignominious', therefore, is the only way to describe the manner in which I was led indoors by the policeman and made to describe, to him and to his superior, my evening dash to the chocolate shop. They listened with barely concealed contempt, and I was given a public dressing down in the hotel reception and told never to try anything like that again (which, surprisingly, I had no immediate plans to do).

'Well, at least I have my chocolates,' I joked as I prepared to make my departure. I had accidentally parted company with them in the flower bed and now looked round to see where they might have been lodged for safekeeping—slightly battered after their collision with a policeman, but yummy all the same.

'I regret to tell you,' said the Inspector, 'that nobody can be allowed to take anything in or out of the hotel. They are confiscated.'

'Confiscated?'

'Yes.'

'All of them?'

'Naturally.'

'But the peach truffle...' I began.

'That is the end of it, *mademoiselle*,' he said. 'You are fortunate not to be charged with a serious crime.'

'But...' I tried not to whimper, but it was difficult. I could put up with incarceration in a hotel with peeling wallpaper. I could put up with a bruising collision with a stationery policeman. I could put up with public humiliation of almost any sort. But no chocolate? Surely the *Code Napoleon* could not have prescribed anything so harsh and unnatural?

It was at this point that Herbie sauntered through the door from the garden. He had clearly profited from my own discomfort and made an easy return over the wall himself while everyone's attention was focussed on me—as may well have been his plan all along. It suddenly struck me that somebody who can land like a cat probably doesn't need to wait for a plastic garden chair to be passed over the wall. I'd been used. He might still have got away with his treachery, but he winked at me conspiratorially as he passed. It was a most ill-advised wink that suggested he thought he was a pretty clever sort of guy. It was a wink that assumed we were in some way still on the same side. It was a most inadvisable wink at a forlorn and chocolate-less literary agent and it was to cost him dearer than he could have ever imagined.

'Just one other thing, Inspector,' I said in a loud voice. 'That man was out there with me.'

Herbie froze on the spot. His eyes looked at me imploringly, but it was too late. Oh dear, it was much too late for that.

'You have certainly just come in from the garden, *Monsieur* Proctor. What exactly were you doing out there?' asked the Inspector with a raised eyebrow.

'I was just sitting out there,' suggested Herbie with more optimism than was justified.

'*C'est vrai?*' These last words were directed by the Inspector at the policeman who had been on guard duty.

'*Je ne l'ai vu point,*' the policeman replied. Having recently been squashed by a petite but rapidly moving literary agent, his view of humanity had changed for the worse. He was not inclined to give people the benefit of the doubt unless it was absolutely necessary.

'My colleague does not seem to recall seeing you. So what have you been up to, *Monsieur* Proctor?' demanded the Inspector.

'You are quite right, Inspector. I did go outside the hotel for a bit,' Herbie said, fiddling with the zip of his fleece. 'I felt like an evening stroll, so I...just climbed over the wall. I merely had a little walk to the bridge and back to work up an appetite. This good lady will confirm what I say, I'm sure.' Again the beseeching eyes in my direction, but peach creams deferred sicken the heart, as Shakespeare once said. There are some things that cannot be forgiven in this life.

'He went to the left luggage office at the railway station,' I said. 'I followed him. He deposited something there in a manner that I can only describe as furtive. You will find the key on him.'

Herbie, who had been looking at me in horror, suddenly smiled as if I had given him a Get Out of Jail Free card. 'She's nuts,' he said. 'I might have walked down towards the station but the rest is rubbish. I've got no key. Search me all you want.'

'Correction,' I said. 'The key is not on him—it's *in* him. He has swallowed it.'

Herbie smiled even more broadly, revealing some unattractive yellow teeth. 'You won't find it inside me either.'

'But I am afraid we shall have to try,' said the Inspector. He turned again to the policeman. 'If you would be so good as to fetch the physician. I think we may need to pump this gentleman's stomach again.'

I'll never forget the look on Herbie Proctor's face as he was led away. I have no idea what his expression was when, a minute or so later, the gong sounded to announce our delicious (and absolutely free) dinner.

CHAPTER 14

It had been a funny sort of day.

After tea, I had retired to the small brown sitting room to think things through, leaving Elsie to make her own way (as I later learned) to the garden.

My own thoughts were not encouraging. That I had been abandoned by a certain party, I now did not doubt. What was unclear was whether the intention had always been to send me on a fool's errand or whether a plausible scheme had been dropped in mid-course without anyone thinking to inform me. Over the past twenty-four hours it had become apparent that all that was left was for me to return to Sussex (or Goa) and await instructions, if any. I was not particularly optimistic that any instructions would be forthcoming.

One of the two remaining bona fide philatelists wandered in apologetically and took the furthest seat from me. I had been introduced to him early on and knew his name was Taylor and his companion was Jones—but that was about all I knew. For a while I had thought of them as Taylor-and-Jones: inseparable and largely indistinguishable. Both were middle-aged. Both wore tweed jackets. Both had lost more hair than they had managed to retain. It was only slowly that they had emerged as individuals, much as twins lose their ability to confuse you as you get to know them better and learn which has the small scar, which the slightly more rounded cheeks. Taylor, I now realised, was the younger of the two by a good ten years and his remaining hair was black rather than grey. Though he may well have patronised the same clothes shops as Jones, his eye was brighter, his jacket was newer, his trousers better pressed, his tie had pretensions to being more than a grubby length of knitted wool from a charity shop. In time, age and misfortune might well turn him into Jones, but for the moment he was still Taylor.

I nodded to him and he nodded back. He sat down in front of a heap of ancient French and English magazines. He picked up and discarded each of them in quick succession and then looked resignedly in my direction. Though we were two strangers, we would just have to talk to each other.

'Nothing to your taste?' I asked, making the first move.

'Nothing I can concentrate on,' said Taylor. His hand ran through some dark strands of hair and then into the pink trackless waste beyond. Ten years too late, he attempted to smooth the tresses on top of his head. 'Like most people here I should have been back at work by now,' he added.

'I suppose I'm lucky in the sense that I can work anywhere,' I said.

He raised an eyebrow.

'I'm a writer,' I said.

'Would I have heard of you?'

'Almost certainly not,' I said. I told him the three pen-names under which I write. As usually happens under these circumstances, the encouraging smile slowly faded into blank indifference.

'So what sort of thing do you write?' Taylor asked, though now with no great display of interest.

'Detective stories mainly,' I said apologetically. 'Maybe not your sort of thing?'

'No, I'm very keen on crime. I read it a lot—Rankin, Grafton, Leonard, Dexter. I just haven't heard of *you*,' he said.

I nodded. It was at least honest.

I expected him to change the subject at this point, but he suddenly looked at me with revived interest.

'So, you'll know all about poisons and so on?' he asked.

This was true. As I say, I know all about poisons, at least theoretically. It's not difficult to gain a superficial knowledge of most things.

'A bit,' I said. 'My readers expect me to know things like that.'

'And how to use them?'

I got the impression I was being interrogated, but was unsure why.

'That's the point of poison—in detective stories, anyway. You use it.'

'You'd know the right dose and everything?'

Yes, this was an interrogation all right. I dearly hoped that Taylor did not see himself in the role of amateur detective.

'I don't murder people in real life,' I said, clarifying exactly what I did. 'It is frequently tempting, but in my books the villains always get caught and are duly punished. Perfect crimes are rare.'

'What about Jack the Ripper?'

'There are exceptions, obviously.'

There was a pause during which I of course had to ask what *he* did. It's pretty unavoidable. Frankly, I had him down as a chemist.

'You might not guess by looking at me, but I'm a chemist,' he said confidentially. 'I work in the soft drinks industry.'

Well, that gave us (including deceased hotel guests) a chemist, a pharmacist and a drug company rep. So it wasn't just the crime writer who might have a knowledge of poisons.

Taylor told me who he worked for. I admitted that the name vaguely rang a bell.

'Yes, we were in the news recently,' he said despondently. 'Somebody was threatening to reveal the formula of our best-selling drink. Of course, any idiot with a toy chemistry set could buy a bottle and analyse it. It's scarcely top secret. But we've made a thing for years about the formula being kept in a locked safe, so we'll look pretty stupid when it's out there for all to see. We'll also look pretty stupid when it's revealed that the secret ingredients are lemon juice, aniseed, caramel syrup and one or two other things you can buy in the supermarket.'

'So what will your people do?'

'Well, I'm just a humble chemist,' he said, 'so I doubt they'll be consulting me. Bearing in mind sales of hundreds of millions of Pounds a year are involved, they may well decide to buy them off. But once stuff like that is out, it's out, isn't it? Short of discreetly murdering these people, there's probably not much we can do.'

He paused, aware that threats of assassination were probably in bad taste under the circumstances.

'Sorry,' he said. 'I didn't mean to suggest the company...or I...'

'Of course,' I said.

'As you say, villains always get caught...'

'In my books anyway,' I said.

It was just starting to get dark outside, when he left and (almost immediately) Mr Proctor put in a brief appearance. I had heard that his 'poisoning' had been a little exaggerated—but he looked ill, as he well might after his treatment.

'Where's tea?' he demanded.

'They cleared it all away ten minutes ago,' I said.

He looked very disappointed.

'I'm sure you could get room service,' I said.

'And they'd charge for that?'

'Possibly. I doubt that it would be exorbitantly expensive.'

He considered this briefly. 'I might get myself some chocolate.'

'I don't think the hotel has any,' I said.

'The shops have.'

'But you can't go out, you know.'

He smiled. 'Herbie Proctor has his methods.'

Only later did I learn that the methods would involve scaling a wall and being pursued on a winter evening by a short, fat literary agent. That was all still in the future and would be related to me over dinner by the agent in question.

'Good luck,' I said, not realising quite how much luck he was going to need.

'Luck's got nothing to do with it,' he replied with a chortle. 'It's all about knowledge and skill. You'll see.'

On my way back to my room, I noticed Elsie carefully carrying a large glass of beer into the garden. But she was too intent on not spilling a single drop to notice me. Yes, it was a funny sort of day.

It was only when I was passing through reception some time later and saw a slightly muddy and bedraggled Elsie being marched in by a red faced policeman that I discovered how much fun everyone else had been having that evening.

If only a message had been left at reception telling me what on earth I was supposed to be doing in Chaubord in the first place, I could have settled back and enjoyed another pleasant evening in the Loire Valley. But there was nothing. Nothing at all.

CHAPTER 15

The news that Herbie Proctor was having his stomach pumped for the second time in one day seemed somehow to cheer everyone up. Hints had also been dropped that this stage of the investigation was almost complete and that we could all check out some time the following morning. Conversation over dinner was lively. Amongst the small group that was left, there was quite a party mood.

Only Ethelred still seemed quite glum.

'Come on,' I said. 'We could be out of here by tomorrow.'

'How do you work that out?' asked Ethelred.

'The police have questioned everyone,' I pointed out.

'But arrested nobody,' he said. 'If there's even a chance that the murderer is amongst us then I don't see how they can let anyone go. Within a few hours everyone here would be out of the country, with the possible exception of the Pedersens, who can probably claim diplomatic immunity anyway.'

'How long can you be detained here without charge?'

'I've no idea. Days? Weeks? Look what happened to the Count of Monte Cristo.'

'In that case,' I said, 'the sooner they arrest somebody the better.'

There was a cough behind me. It was the nice policeman that I had jumped on earlier.

'*Mademoiselle* Thirkettle,' he said—rather formally, I thought, for somebody that I had been so close to—'I regret to inform you that we need to ask you some more questions.'

'I was about to order dessert,' I said.

'I am afraid this cannot wait.'

'You'll have to arrest me to keep me away from the profiteroles,' I joked.

'That was my intention,' he said. 'I think it would be better if you accompanied me without further fuss.'

The police had taken over one of the back offices, an untidy room made untidier by the numerous half-finished mugs of coffee and dirty plates that had accumulated there. I was offered the less well-padded of the two chairs in the room. The Inspector took the comfy one. He seemed friendlier than the policeman, possibly because I had not recently landed on top of him, forcing his face into the freezing flowerbed.

'*Mademoiselle* Thirkettle,' he said, 'I think you may not have been entirely truthful with us.'

He paused, leaving me to wonder which of the lies I had told recently he was referring to. Since he would have no idea what an English Size 10 looked like, it was improbable that he would be picking me up on that. Maybe it was the one about never having gone into Grigory Davidov's room? Hmm, I'd just have to wait and see. In the interim, I tried the same sweet smile that I had tried in the flowerbed.

'Could you tell me, for example, why we found your fingerprints in *Monsieur* Davidov's room?' asked the Inspector.

The answer to the question was of course that I thought they must have already dusted for fingerprints well before I went in there, otherwise I might have been a bit more careful. They'd fingerprinted all of the hotel guests earlier so it would not have taken them long to work out who had been eating whose chocolate.

'I just thought I'd take a look round,' I said. It didn't sound any more convincing when I said it than it does written down. At the best I sounded like some sort of peeping Tom. At the worst I was the poison queen of Chaubord sur Loire. Obviously one of these was marginally better than the other.

'A look round?' he said, spitting the words out one by one. Clearly, in his view, poisoners ranked slightly above peeping Toms.

'The door just sort of came open,' I said, trying hard not to sound either weird or criminal this time. 'After I'd unlocked it, that is. So I sort of wandered in to look for chocolate and ended up going through his dressing gown pockets… I'm not explaining this very well, am I?'

'We are of course aware that you took away the box of chocolate truffles, because we recovered it from your room. Why did you take them?'

'You can't search my room just like that.'

'Yes, we can.'

Fair enough.

'Well, what do *you* think anyone would want to do with a box of chocolates?' I said.

If I could just pause for a moment and give you some advice—never try irony on British traffic wardens, US immigration officials or French policemen. For some reason, none of them get it. None of them.

The Inspector did not smile. 'And you ate them all?'

'Every last one. Is that a crime?'

'It did not occur to you that this might be dangerous?' asked the Inspector.

'Not at that moment in time. It did occur to me shortly before I sicked up in the bushes, but not when I was actually eating them. Unfortunately.'

'At least, *Mademoiselle* Thirkettle, you have saved us checking whether the others were also poisoned. We could regard that as a service to the French state perhaps.'

'Do I get the Legion of Honour?'

'No,' he said. (See above comments on irony.)

'Did you handle the box?' he asked.

'Yes,' I said. 'Of course I did.'

'A lot?'

'There was a lot of chocolate.'

'That would explain,' he said, 'why the only fingerprints we can identify on the box are yours.'

He looked at me. I looked at him. He looked at me.

'Is that it?' I asked, hopefully.

'No, that isn't it,' he said. 'Did you go into *Monsieur* Davidov's room at any other time?'

'What on earth for?'

'Somebody suggested that you might have done.'

'Do you mean Herbie Proctor?' I asked. The light suddenly dawned.

'Of course, we would have checked the room for your finger-prints anyway,' he said.

Yes, daylight dawned, but it was a nasty, creepy, grey dawn.

'The filthy, lying toe-rag!' I observed calmly.

'On the contrary, our informant was absolutely on the nose, as you say.'

'It's just because I grassed him up about the key...' I began.

'Grassed up? You mean...?'

'Told you he had the key.'

'Ah, and that is *grassed up*. I shall make a note. You are assuming, of course, that our informant was indeed *Monsieur* Proctor,' said the Inspector. 'By the way, he had not swallowed a key.'

'No?'

'No. We x-rayed his stomach in the hospital. No metal objects of any kind.'

'Well, he's a very suspicious character for all that,' I said. 'Why don't you try pumping his stomach just one more time?'

The Inspector smiled. 'I think not.'

'Shame,' I said. 'But he did have a key.'

'He says not.'

'What you have to do,' I said, 'is to search all of the left luggage lockers for the thing he has hidden there.'

'Which is what?'

'I don't know,' I said.

'So—I am curious to find this out—how will we know when we find it?'

'It will be a suspicious object,' I said.

'Did you see him carrying anything with him on the way to the station?'

I thought back to his cat-like leap from the wall. A bag would have been very noticeable. 'No,' I said, 'but...'

'So, this is just a guess on your part?'

'Yes,' I said, 'but...'

'*Mademoiselle* Thirkettle,' he said, leaning forward and narrowing his eyes, 'you seem determined to cast suspicion upon yourself in every possible way. In future, please stay out of police investigations. Please, do not try to climb the garden wall— and certainly not in that skirt. Please do not make accusations against your fellow guests unless you have something remotely resembling evidence. Please do not eat or otherwise interfere with any evidence. And, above all, please do not jump on any of my police officers. They do not like it; it makes them feel uncomfortable. Is that clear?'

I wondered if I should tell him how sexy he looked when he narrowed his eyes like that, but I just said demurely: 'But of course, *Monsieur* Inspector.'

'In fact, just stay completely out of the way until we tell you that you can go.'

'Am I under arrest?'

'You are very fortunate not to be.'

'Am I free to return to the dining room?'

'Or to any other room, except the room of the late *Monsieur* Davidov.'

I sprinted back down the corridor, but met Ethelred and the others as they were leaving their tables.

'You missed some great profiteroles,' said Ethelred.

'Are there any left?' I asked.

'No,' said Ethelred. 'They've just stopped serving.'

'I had seconds,' observed one of the Danish children gleefully. He was saved from justifiable infanticide only by one thing. Herbie Proctor was just behind me. He looked a bit like a famine relief advertisement, but not so deserving.

'Any food left?' he asked desperately.

I smiled. Sometimes it's those small, simple things that can really make your day.

CHAPTER 16

Stabbing somebody to death is easier than you would think. Agatha Christie complicates things a little in *Murder on the Orient Express* by having some of the victim's wounds as mere scratches, that being the most the perpetrator could manage. A stab wound does not in fact require a great deal of force. Once the knife has penetrated the skin, surprisingly little effort is required to make a deep wound.

Wounds can however be remarkably variable. The shape of the weapon will affect the shape of the wound, and the wound from a double-edged knife is often said to be very different from that of a single edged knife. The blunt side of a knife can however split the skin in a way that looks very much like a cut from a sharp edge, so you shouldn't believe everything you read. Much depends too on whether the cut is in the direction of Langer's Lines or perpendicular to them. Those parallel to Langer's Lines will usually be slit-like—those at right angles will gape open.

The size of the wound will be increased if the knife is rocked or twisted in the wound. The latter is referred to in the street parlance of South London as a 'juke'.

One peculiarity of knife wounds is that they can actually be longer than the weapon inflicting them. This is because of the compression of the skin and underlying tissue as the blow is struck. Conversely the width of a stab wound is usually less than the width of the knife because the skin will contract around the wound. A superficial examination of a stab wound can therefore sometimes be misleading.

A certain amount of evidence can be gained, if the victim is unable to communicate, from the pattern of defence wounds—cuts to the hands and forearms are usually sustained in trying to fend off or actually grasp the blade.

Stabbings tend to be by young men and perpetrated on young men, but women will use a knife in the heat of the moment. One Margaret Williams, for example, stabbed her husband twice and got lucky on the second attempt, penetrating the heart. His last words were apparently, 'You think I am scared of a little knife?'

Stabbings are rarer in detective fiction than in real life. Perhaps writers consider them inelegant, though Christie employs stabbing in a number of classics—not only *Murder on the Orient Express*, but also *Death on the Nile* and (perhaps her finest work of all) the *Murder of Roger Ackroyd*.

In my capacity as a writer of historical detective fiction my characters inevitably stumble across a range of stab wounds. Interestingly, however, we have added fewer new methods of murder over the intervening years than you might imagine: firearms, electrocution, bombs, hit and run driving. But sharp and blunt instruments, strangling, poison, drowning and suffocation are timeless. There are ways in which murder is quite familiar and reassuring.

CHAPTER 17

I had been forbidden to interfere in police investigations, but that (surely?) could not include having friendly chats with hotel staff. Particularly not receptionists, who are likely to get lonely during the long hours after dinner...and who may wish to relive, with a nice, sympathetic literary agent (say), the events of the night they were on duty and a fatal stabbing occurred.

Accordingly I drifted out of the bar clutching my Perrier, and over towards the reception desk. The receptionist was sitting hunched over a newspaper. He was completing some sort of number puzzle, chewing a short stub of pencil contemplatively. He wore a cheap black jacket, white shirt and thin black tie with much the same ill grace as I once wore my school uniform. There was a small white badge pinned to his lapel. It looked like the sort of badge you get as waste-paper monitor, but this one said: 'Jean-Luc'. A stale aroma of blighted hopes hung around him. One day soon he would look in the mirror and notice his hair was starting to turn grey and he would try to remember why he had thought it such a good plan to become a hotel receptionist.

He looked up as he heard me approach, and pushed his number puzzle to one side, but not so far that it was out of reach.

I smiled sweetly and began to strike up a friendly conversation.

'You work long hours,' I said.

Jean-Luc looked at me blankly. '*Mais, oui,*' he said.

'Poor you,' I said, as if he were a novelist who had just had his book rejected by the tenth publisher in a row.

'It is normal—in this business,' said Jean-Luc, but he seemed pleased I had noticed, as hotel staff often do.

'Have you worked here long?'

'Since I was twenty,' he said.

So that was maybe twenty or twenty five years ago?

'So that would be about fifteen years ago,' I said. Even men (contrary to what they tell you) are susceptible to a little flattery about their age.

He gave a pleased sort of shrug. 'A little longer, maybe.'

'Your family...your *young* family...must find it inconvenient?'

He nodded. 'But it is normal,' he said. 'Normal in this *métier.*'

So—a fairly regular sort of guy, a long-serving employee, a family man. Not a likely murderer, surely?

'You certainly have a lot of stamp collectors here,' I observed, trying to work the conversation imperceptibly towards asking him if he ever killed guests.

'Stamp collectors?' he said.

'Yes, stamp collectors,' I said.

'It is the *Stamp Fair,*' he said as though explaining something very simple to somebody who was very simple. 'There are naturally the stamp collectors.'

'And a lot of your regulars are back?' I asked.

He shook his head. 'I don't think any of the guests—any of the guests who are still here—were with us for the fair last year,' he said.

'So you hadn't met Jonathan Gold before?'

'No.'

'Or Grigory Davidov?'

'I'd heard of him, of course.'

'And you don't approve of the way he conducts business?'

'It is not my affair. They say he wants to buy your Manchester United. I think you are crazy to sell your football teams to foreigners. If I supported Manchester United I would not be too happy.'

I nodded and made a mental note to ask Ethelred to explain football to me some time.

'And the other guests? What about them?'

He shrugged, and I tended to agree with him. What was there to know about them?

'Well, with so many stamp collectors around, I was lucky to get a room, then.'

'It is safer to book when the stamp fair is on,' he said. 'Most of the other guests had booked well in advance, except you.'

'Most?'

He glanced quickly at his computer screen. '*Monsieur* Tressider of course made your reservation. Everyone else seems to have booked themselves.'

There was something not right with this last piece of information, but at first I couldn't quite put my finger on it. Then I could.

'Including *Monsieur* Brown?' I said.

Jean-Luc sighed and looked again at the screen. 'Including *Monsieur* Brown. He reserved some weeks ago by email.'

So—this was the thing that was not right—Brown had clearly lied to me about this being a last minute decision. I promoted him, immediately and deservedly, to Number One Suspect. But that meant there was something more I needed to know. Brown had been suspiciously absent from dinner.

'What time did he get back on his first evening here?' I asked.

'Get back?' asked the receptionist.

'After he had gone out.'

'I don't remember seeing him at all that evening.'

'What time did you go off duty?'

'I am on duty during all of the night. There is nobody else. I stay on duty until after breakfast.' The receptionist paused and then added: 'Can you tell *me* something?'

'I'll try.'

'Why do you all ask me so many questions?'

'All?'

'You. *Monsieur* Taylor. *Monsieur* Smith. *Monsieur* Proctor. *Monsieur* Tressider. Do you all play at detectives?'

'Some are playing, Jean-Luc,' I said, 'some aren't.'

He shook his head. 'I think you are all...how do you say?... weirdoes.'

'Are you calling me a weirdo?'

'Frankly, *mademoiselle*, yes.' He reached over and pulled his number puzzle back towards him. He retrieved his pencil. 'Is there anything else?'

I wondered whether this was the point at which I should tell him that (frankly) he did not look a day under fifty, but I decided that could wait. So I thanked him with studied politeness and moved on.

But I could see why the police had ruled him out as a suspect. He was an unlikely murderer. He seemed to have no previous connection with either victim and was more worried about the impact of Davidov's money on the Premiership than his annihilation of a medium sized town in India. And, in any case, why would he risk killing somebody at his own place of work?

I went back to the bar to think just a little bit more about Mr Brown.

Ethelred was already there, drinking a calvados with his coffee. I told him what I discovered about Brown. He did not seem impressed.

'That doesn't make him a murderer,' he said.

'But why should he lie about the booking?' I asked. 'Why didn't he just say it was a long drive, so he booked a room here to break the journey? Why pretend it was all by chance?'

'So, which one did he kill? Gold or Davidov?'

'Either or both,' I suggested.

'But he had no links with them as far as we know.'

'He is in the pharmaceutical industry. Gold was a pharmacist of some sort.'

'Keep going. There are a surprising number of people here who know at least a little about drugs. What makes him stand out?'

'You have to admit that somebody in the pharmaceutical industry would have access to poisons.'

'You told me he had no drugs with him,' said Ethelred reasonably.

'If he'd stuck them all in the peach truffle, then he wouldn't have,' I said.

Ethelred grinned, the way men grin to indicate that they've got a big male brain and you've just got a pathetic little female brain. I had to remind myself that I'd already murdered him once this year, which was probably as often as I could get away with. Still, there was always next year to look forward to.

'He arrived just before Davidov was poisoned,' I said. 'He was keener than anyone to get away afterwards. And where was he all night?'

'Maybe he didn't go out. Maybe he had supper at some service station before he even got to the hotel. Maybe he just decided to have an early night. Or maybe he did go out to some little bistro in town and when he came back the receptionist did not see him. Even receptionists have to go and pee sometimes.'

'I think he poisoned Davidov,' I said. 'He has the knowledge of poisons. Nobody knows where he was all night. And he tells porkies.'

'But,' said Ethelred, 'he doesn't have a motive for either killing—or none that we know of.'

'You don't think he could commit a murder?' I asked.

'Anyone could commit murder,' said Ethelred with a sigh. 'You just have to be angry enough or frightened enough at the wrong time. Now, I think I might have another small calvados, then I'm off to bed.'

There's nothing quite as dull as being confined to a hotel with peeling wall-paper during a Police investigation that you are not allowed to interfere with in any way at all. People tended to move from one room to another to relieve the boredom of it all. I waited in the stuffy little sitting room. Sure enough, Tim Brown eventually drifted by.

I hadn't noticed how blond he was. That should have made him halfway good-looking, but, great hair apart, he was pretty ordinary—early thirties, medium height, a bit overweight from too many three course dinners on the road and too many beers in the bar afterwards. He was still wearing the rather creased jacket and trousers, but they were a bit more creased than when I last noticed him. He looked tired and more than a little worried. Time for some more subtle questioning, but this time in a way that would not make me look like a junkie needing a fix.

'Nice meal tonight,' I said.

'Yes,' he said.

'The food was good here last night too, wasn't it?'.

'It was fine.'

'But you didn't eat here last night,' I pointed out.

Clearly he had hoped to avoid the subject.

'No, I found a little restaurant in town,' he said, looking at the nearest magazine.

'Which one?'

'I don't really remember,' he said, picking up the magazine and starting to flick through the pages. He was holding it upside down, but he hadn't noticed that yet.

'Quick service?'

He frowned and looked up at me. 'I don't quite understand...'

'Service can be quite slow in France. It's really irritating when you just want to get back to the hotel and off to bed after a long day, then you're kept waiting for ever for the bill, don't you find?'

'No, the service was perfectly OK. I don't understand what you are getting at.'

'What I am getting at is: how come you were out all night? That would be the slowest service I've ever come across.'

OK, forget what I said about subtle questioning.

The magazine fell to the floor with a loud plop.

'Who says I didn't come back?'

'Jean-Luc, the receptionist.'

He scowled. Well, that was one prematurely-aged member of the hotel staff who would not be getting a tip from our Mr Brown.

'Yes,' he said thoughtfully. 'Perhaps, service was a little slower than I would have liked.'

'All night?'

'I went for a walk afterwards. I didn't feel tired.'

'I said: all *night*?'

'It's an interesting town.'

'That sounds a bit unlikely, especially after a long drive up from Bordeaux.'

'Er...' said the poor male creature in front of me.

'Do you want to just tell me everything?' I asked. 'It will be easier in the long run.'

'Are you a private detective?' he asked.

I smiled enigmatically. Putty in my hands? That was an understatement.

'Shit,' he said. 'OK. This was bound to happen sooner or later. Where do you want me to start?'

'Were you planning to kill Gold all along?' I asked, striking home with deadly accuracy.

'Gold?' he asked, bewildered.

'I mean Davidov,' I said, striking home in a slightly different, but equally good, way. 'When exactly did you decide to poison Davidov, Mr Brown?'

'Davidov?'

Pretending he had not heard of his victims (if that was the plan) was not going to do him much good at this stage.

'How did you get the poison in the chocolate? Did you inject it? You may as well fess up,' I asked.

He gave me that old familiar you're-a-weirdo look.

'Let's get this straight: you're accusing me of murdering either Gold or Davidov?' he said, the penny beginning to drop in his small male brain.

'That's right,' I said.

He gave a relieved chuckle. 'Is that all?' he said.

Murder? It seemed plenty to be going on with. 'Yes,' I said.

'Thank goodness for that,' he laughed. He looked like the most relieved man in the Loire Valley. 'And I thought...'

'You thought...?' I said, still hoping he might be about to crumble and confess all.

He stood up. 'Good night, Ms Thirkettle,' he said. 'I rather think I'll turn in. As you say, it was a long drive yesterday.'

'Do the Police know you were out all night?' I asked. A final shot at blackmail seemed worthwhile.

'Yes,' he said. 'I told them.'

'Ah,' I said. 'That's OK then.'

After he'd gone, I tidied away the magazine he had dropped on the floor and straightened some of the cushions. Then I went to bed too. I noted Ethelred was still in the bar, cradling his glass, but I didn't think it was worth reporting back on my conversation with Tim Brown.

Ethelred was already smug enough without that.

I noticed a couple of things when I got back to my room. The policeman who had been guarding Davidov's room had gone, suggesting that they'd checked it out it as much as they were planning to. Second, as I opened my own door, I noticed that my light was on and that I hadn't needed my key to get in. I was pretty sure I'd switched the light off before going down to dinner. And surely I had locked the door? Possibly, I thought, the maid had been in to turn the bed down or put a little chocolate surprise on my pillow. But no—the bed was in much the same state as before. No night-time chocolate treat. Everything was much as before, in fact. It was true that, the way I'd left things before dinner, it would have been difficult to establish that the room had been ransacked, but I could at least be sure that nobody had broken in and tidied up.

I walked cautiously over to the window and looked out across the dark street to the blank wall of the chateau grounds. The street was deserted and the lights made everything look pale and bloodless. Rain was starting to fall. I waited for a car to pass, but the street stayed empty.

I drew the curtains together, expecting it to make the room feel cosy, but somehow it didn't. I locked the door, expecting to feel safer, but I felt just as before. When I went to the bathroom to clean my teeth I left the door open and kept my eye on the room in the mirror—I didn't want someone, or some Thing, creeping up on me.

I changed into my pyjamas. They were of the warm and comfortable variety rather than the ones you normally wear for seducing Brad Pitt, but it seemed unlikely he would show up, so I could risk the elasticated waistband and the pink bunny pattern.

When I was a little girl, I had a firm rule that once you were safely in bed, the bogeyman could not get you. Whether the bogeyman also recognised this rule I can't say. Strangely, that evening, even once I was in bed, I still did not feel safe. Of course, you only get 100% bogeyman protection if you pull the blankets right over your head.

I switched the light off, pulled the duvet right over me and tried to sleep.

CHAPTER 18

'I'm no closer to cracking the case,' I said.

'Nobody is asking you to crack it,' said Ethelred. 'Just leave it uncracked. That's fine.'

'But I can't help feeling the answer is staring us in the face,' I said.

Ethelred smiled. I hadn't even told him about the Tim Brown incident and he was still a bit too smug for my liking. Well, we'd see who got the last laugh.

We were sitting in an otherwise empty dining room, enjoying a solitary breakfast, nobody else having chosen to get up at stupid o'clock. In the massive stone fireplace, last night's ashes were cold and as yet untouched. Coffee had been slow to arrive and the pot was only half full when it did.

'Not as lavish as yesterday,' I observed, searching the bread-basket in vain for a *pain au chocolat*.

'No,' said Ethelred. 'I think that the hotel is beginning to repent its earlier generosity now investigations are extending into a second day. Apparently there will be sandwiches free of charge at lunchtime, but anything else will have to be paid for at the usual rates.'

'Herbie won't be too happy about that,' I said.

Ethelred took a bite out of his (non-chocolate) breakfast pastry.

'So, how far have you got?' he asked.

'I've ruled out the hotel staff,' I said. 'Well, actually the Police seem to have ruled them out, in that they are now apparently free to come and go, whereas we are here.'

Ethelred shrugged. 'The manager was away from early evening until the following morning. Jean-Luc, the receptionist, has no clear motive and swears that, unusually, none of the other staff were there that night. All staff have, obviously, been questioned, but it's difficult to see why any of them should kill two guests, especially when the second murder was, as we have agreed, a pretty risky business.'

'So, it's back to the guests,' I said. 'One of whom was desperate to cover up something.'

'Perhaps,' said Ethelred, 'Davidov did kill Gold.'

'You were a bit dismissive of that when it was my theory,' I said.

'So, it's not your theory now?'

'They clearly knew each other,' I said. 'Something was going on between them. We know that Davidov went over to London. I think it must have been to meet Gold in that kosher restaurant— but Gold stood him up.'

'Not necessarily.'

'How else do you explain the receipt in Davidov's dressing gown pocket? Tell me that. And don't you dare shrug.'

'You could be right,' Ethelred conceded graciously, but his shoulders twitched a bit as he said it. 'All we really know, though, is that Davidov was in London shortly before he was killed. We don't know that he met Gold.'

'OK,' I said, 'But I do think that Davidov's death and the theft of his envelope are connected. Somebody poisoned Davidov and stole whatever was in the safe.'

Ethelred shook his head. 'Somebody stole Davidov's valuable envelope and poisoned him.'

'That's what I said.'

'My point,' said the annoying possessor of the large male brain, 'is that the envelope was stolen *first*. Davidov was at reception complaining about the theft shortly before he died. If stealing the envelope was the motive, why hang around to kill him? Why not make a run for it while you can? Alternatively, if the primary aim was to kill him, why risk having the police called in to investigate a stolen envelope?'

This was such a good point that I decided to change the subject.

'There are some of the guests that we can rule out as Davidov's killer,' I said. 'Tim Brown, for a start.'

'I thought you suspected him because he told porkies?'

'Yes, but I tricked him into telling me a bit more,' I said, giving selected highlights only of my discussion with him. 'I discovered why he was out all night.'

'He told you?'

'Sort of. He was really worried when he thought I was a private detective.'

'I see...' Ethelred looked unnecessarily dubious. 'And why did he think you were a private eye?'

'He just did,' I said. 'Now, who would send a private detective after him? Answer using words. Don't shrug.'

'I wasn't planning to shrug. Who would spy on him? I don't know...a competitor? A business partner? His wife?'

'His wife...exactly! Brown goes to the conference. All the time he has planned, on his way back home, to stop off here and meet up with some floozy...'

Ethelred held up his hand. He was not taking this as seriously as he should.

'Is this the same floozy you accuse me of consorting with?'

'Don't be a dickhead,' I said.

'I just wanted to check. You don't see that many floozies these days. I think they went out of fashion in the early sixties. Or possibly even the late fifties. I think their natural habitat was the boudoir, which few houses now have.'

'Brown seems a normal sensible man,' I said, pre-empting further speculation on the natural history of the floozy, 'but then he does something weird—that is to say he stops off in a grotty hotel to rest up and vanishes for the entire night. It is a clear case of a man whose brain is firmly in his trousers. I have no doubt that a lady friend of his similarly broke her journey in another hotel with peeling wallpaper, and that is the hotel in which they both spent the night. The moment he thought that I was a detective, his guilty conscience immediately assumed I had been sent by his wife to tail him around town. Whatever he's done, it's not murder.'

'If you say so,' said Ethelred.

'You can forget Howard Taylor too.'

'He seems to be investigating Davidov's murder in a private capacity,' said Ethelred. 'He also seems to be a devotee of detective fiction.'

'A fan of yours?'

'Apparently not,' he said.

Ethelred took another bite of his brioche.

'But why are you so sure it couldn't be Taylor?' he asked.

'Too spineless, even for poison.'

'You can't spot a murderer by casual inspection,' he said.

'As for the Danish family, if you are going to murder somebody, you'd hardly bring the kids along for the ride,' I said.

'Unless you were being very clever,' said Ethelred. 'I think one of Sue Grafton's hitmen does something of the sort. So, who knows?'

I looked at him to see if was joking. He was. I think.

'That leaves Herbie Proctor and Taylor's tweedy friend,' I said.

'Ah yes, John Jones,' said Ethelred. 'I've hardly spoken to him. He doesn't talk to anyone much.'

'A man of mystery,' I said.

'A man devoid of mystery or anything else,' said Ethelred. 'A genuine stamp collector. A friend of Taylor's. I saw them both snooping around together playing at detectives. One of them actually used the phrase 'my little grey cells', if you can believe that.'

I believed that.

'So, it's Herbie then,' I concluded. 'A born poisoner if ever I saw one. And he was desperate to sneak something out of the hotel.'

'But with no really good motive for murdering Davidov,' said Ethelred, 'or Gold for that matter.'

'Hang on,' I said. 'Gold told me he knew Proctor.'

'In what capacity?'

'I don't know—it was just a passing remark. He told me that he had seen him before.'

'So, he can't have known him well?' said Ethelred.

'Presumably not.'

We both thought about this for a while.

'So, nobody is under suspicion then?' I said.

'As far as Gold is concerned, I'm beginning to think it has to be Davidov—I just don't understand why. As far as Davidov is concerned, I think everyone is under suspicion, me included. Oligarchs tend to have enemies. Davidov, particularly after the Yacoubabad disaster, was disliked by more than most. It's said he's had people killed when they crossed him. I'm just surprised that no one chose to lace his chocolate with cyanide before now.'

'Maybe we're concentrating on the wrong thing,' I said. 'If we just knew what was in the envelope...'

'Yes,' said Ethelred, suddenly very thoughtful. 'But we don't.'

'Ethelred,' I said. 'Do *you* know what was in it?'

'No,' he said.

'You're not keeping something back?'

'I've no idea what was in the envelope,' he said. 'I wish I did.'

'Just as long as you are telling me everything.'

'Absolutely,' he said.

'But this envelope has to be the key to it all. I bet that was what Herbie had got his hands on and was trying to hide.'

'But how?' asked the ever-reasonable Ethelred.

'I don't know,' I said, 'Nor do I know who committed the murders. But I'd still like Herbie Proctor to be sufficiently involved to have his stomach pumped again. Is that really too much to ask?'

After breakfast, Ethelred went off to take a stroll round the garden and I decided to hang around in dark corners in the hope of overhearing private conversations. Strangely I chanced on an interesting one straightaway. It was Tim Brown clearly concluding a conversation on his mobile phone.

'Anyway, I'm sorry I missed your call earlier,' he was saying. 'Reception is pretty patchy in this hotel.'

He listened to a brief response from the other end.

'Well, I hope the police didn't give you a hard time,' he added. 'I'm really grateful you were able to confirm I was with you all night at your hotel.'

There was a pause as he listened to the floozy at the other end, then he said: 'That's right. There's this interfering little female here—you know the type? God, she's a pain in the prover-bial. Well, did *she* jump to the wrong conclusion! Fortunately she's got no way of guessing what was going on and doesn't have the brains to work it out.'

'Oh, right,' I thought. 'That's all you and your floozy know.'

'So, I'll see you back in London,' he was saying. 'Yes—me too—can't wait. It's time to come out and tell them all, I think.'

So he was about to leave his wife for the Other Woman?

'Bye, Ian,' he concluded, and snapped the phone shut.

Ian? His wife had more than one shock coming then.

CHAPTER 19

I number fictional characters amongst my closest friends.

In the year or so that it takes to write a book, you get to know your cast quite well—their physical appearance, the sound of their voices, their strange superstitions and prejudices. Sergeant Fairfax, as the hero of eight books of mine, was somebody I got to know better than most. What I really liked about him was that he was a miserable bastard without a single good expectation for the future. He had the ability to radiate gloom amongst his underlings and superiors alike. I don't mean that he had no sense of humour, but it was the sort of humour that can be expressed only through a twisted mouth. His jokes were the sort of jokes that the Tommies probably told each other as they went over the top, white-faced, bayonets fixed, for their first and last time. They were the sort of one-liners that would occur to you as you mounted the scaffold.

But on whom was he based? People often asked me and I was never able to say. There must have been a starting point—a moment when I first saw him emerging, as it were, through the mist of creation, still only half formed and perhaps still with a good word to say about somebody or something. But I know his first recorded words were: 'Bring me some decent coffee, Stepney; this stuff's shit!' I also made them the last words he spoke in my latest—my final—Buckfordshire novel. The cover had announced 'The eighth Sergeant Fairfax murder mystery'. One day, perhaps, the cover will bear the words 'The final Sergeant Fairfax murder mystery'. I am not planning to write another. I doubt that the reading public will notice.

What I fear is that, as I examine my characters one by one, I shall conclude that they all derive from one single source: myself. I am in every sense the father of my creations. Each character I send into the world carries with them a portion of my DNA. Each betrays a little more than I would wish about how I think, how I act, how I am. Each novel is a public confession of my faults.

But, if that is so, then how have I also created Master Thomas—late fourteenth century sleuth and clerk to the obnoxious windbag Geoffrey Chaucer? His bright and beady-eyed determination to see good in everybody strikes no chord in me at all. As he struggles to uncover the truth, hampered alike by his master and the complete absence of mediaeval forensic science, he is never downhearted, never beaten. I always give the Master Thomas books a happy ending—it's the least I can do for him. I'm also going to kill Chaucer in the nastiest way I can find. I might slip Master Thomas some strychnine just to see what he does with it.

And where did the name 'Fairfax' come from? One moment a character has no name, the next they are irrevocably who they are. But 'Fairfax' was absolutely right, with its overtones of puritan rectitude and undeniable Englishness. He never could be anything else. And why did I chance on 'Stepney' for his much put-upon sidekick? I could have called him 'Smith' or 'Brown' or something equally anonymous. It is not—as some critics have speculated—that it is because he is stepped on so much by Fairfax. It was only when writing the third Fairfax book that I remembered a bully at school named Stepney. And it was towards the end of the third book that Stepney suffered the humiliation of letting a prisoner escape and being tied to a railing with his own handcuffs.

Of course, sometimes you will realise that a name is wrong or that somebody else has used the name. One of my minor characters was called 'Roger Ackroyd' for a short time, until a glance along my bookshelves put me right. My editor sometimes insisted on a late change when he thought two characters had similar names. As a rule of thumb, I'd say don't have two major characters beginning with the same letter of the alphabet—as Elsie often points out to me, the sort of people who read my books get easily flustered.

Elsie and I were sitting down to lunch, when Herbie Proctor marched into the dining room. We had already ordered and been served with some ham sandwiches from the 'free' menu. The adequate *vin ordinaire* was also complimentary. I had, in my card-less state, steered clear of the *a la carte* menu, which looked pricy.

I wondered whether Proctor had heard that the hotel's charging policy had changed since the day before. Elsie echoed my thoughts.

'Do you think he's heard?' she said.

'Oh, he must have done,' I said.

'It's just,' said Elsie, 'that it would be so awkward for him if he hadn't.'

We turned to look at him with interest.

'Right, Pierre,' he was saying to the waiter. 'There's a free lunch again is there? Absolutely gratis?'

The waiter nodded. 'Perhaps I can show you the sandwich menu...' he began.

'Not for me,' said Proctor, puffing out his little chest.

'There is also the *a la carte*,' said the waiter caressingly turning the page in Proctor's leather-covered menu.

'Thank you, *garçon*,' said Proctor, possibly noticing the waiter's new tone of respect. 'That looks more the ticket. I'll have the *pâté de fois gras*, followed by the largest steak you can fit on the plate. Then I'll think about afters.'

'Of course, sir,' said the waiter.

'Now, wine,' said Proctor. 'Is that being done on the same basis as the food?'

'As the food you have just ordered?'

'Obviously, Pierre, obviously,' said Proctor, nose in the wine list.

'Naturally, sir.'

Proctor's index finger ran quickly down the page to where I knew the hotel's choicest wines dwelt in relatively undisturbed splendour. I had glanced at them longingly more than once, as must many another guests.

Proctor stabbed his finger in the painfully expensive sector of the page.

'I'll have a bottle of that one,' he said.

'Certainly, sir,' breathed the waiter, deeply impressed.

As he departed, Proctor winked at me. 'Just a sandwich for you two?'

'Yes,' I said.

'Been stuffing yourself with the free grub too much,' he said.

I agreed that we had eaten well up to this point.

'I'm looking forward to this,' said Proctor.

We watched him eat, enjoying each mouthful with him. It was as well that he had no premonition of what each mouthful was costing. We left shortly before the waiter arrived with the bill. It would have been fun to watch, but sometimes these things are better left to the imagination.

CHAPTER 20

It was a sad and thoughtful Herbie Proctor who entered the sitting room in search of a post-lunch coffee.

'Did you know they were charging for everything except sandwiches?' he demanded.

'Were they?' I said. If I had had butter in my mouth at that moment it would not have melted—not even if it was the sort that spreads straight from the fridge. 'We just had sandwiches.'

'You just had sandwiches?' He looked at me suspiciously.

'I wasn't that hungry.'

'And Ethelred?'

'Not what you would call a big eater.' I fluttered my eyelashes a little, rather as Shirley Temple might have done under similar circumstances.

'Have you got something in your eye?' he said.

'No,' I said.

'You could have warned me,' he said.

'So I could,' I said.

He appeared to consider this, and a sort of smile crossed his weasely face. 'Look, maybe you and I got off on the wrong foot,' he said, rancid cooking oil dripping from every word. 'As I said to you once before: aren't we after the same thing here?'

'I am sure, Mr Proctor, that I have no idea what you are talking about,' I said, loftily.

'Yes you do,' he said, with rather greater accuracy. 'Perhaps I might suggest we combine forces rather than fight against each other. It would be easier for you and, it would seem, cheaper for me.'

An alliance with a weasel was a new idea. I was inclined to be cautious.

'What exactly are you after?' I asked.

Though we both knew that the small sitting room was empty except for the two of us, Herbie Proctor made a great show of looking round for the room for possible eavesdroppers before he said: 'It's the Danish stamps.'

'The ten kroner puces?' I said.

'That's right,' he said. 'I'm here to track them down.'

'Why?'

He ferreted in one of his pockets and produced a rather battered card, which he handed to me. It read: 'Proctor and Proctor: all types of private investigative work including divorce and matrimonial'.

'Which Proctor are you?' I asked.

'Both,' he said. 'It's a small agency.'

'So, who are you working for?'

He looked at me, as if uncertain whether I could be trusted with the information.

'You can trust me,' I said with a friendly smile.

He looked even more uncertain, then said very quickly: 'Mr Andersen…Mr H C Andersen. Sorry—I shouldn't really have told you that.'

I nodded encouragingly. This time he seemed reassured. I was obviously getting better at this.

'As you know,' he continued, 'the stamps were…lost shall we say?…at a flea market in Nykøbing. My client, Mr Andersen, is the rightful owner. I discovered that the persons who had acquired the stamps intended to sell them here to a rich and not very scrupulous collector before ownership could be contested in the courts. That collector was Mr Davidov.'

He paused so that I could say 'crikey!' or 'cripes!' or something similar, but I just gave him half a nod on account.

'And who was selling?'

'The Pedersens,' he said. 'A bit coincidental their turning up here in the middle of winter on a family holiday, don't you think? They'd come to sell the stamps.'

'He's a diplomat at the Danish Embassy,' I pointed out.

'Not he,' said Proctor. 'I phoned the Embassy up. There's no such person there. It's all a put up job.'

'Really?' I said. Actually, the Pedersens *had* seemed a bit too good to be true. There was perhaps at least a kernel of truth in what he was saying. 'So, where are the stamps now?'

'The Pedersens sold them to Davidov—that was what was in his envelope. Then somebody stole them from him. I reckon the Pedersens ended up with both the stamps and the bunce. They probably counted on Davidov not going to the police to try to recover stamps he could not admit to owning.'

'Then who killed Davidov?'

Proctor shrugged. 'Not my problem,' he said. 'Don't care, either. I'm only after the stamps. But Davidov had lots of enemies.'

'Did he?' I said.

Proctor looked at me pityingly. 'Do you ever read the papers?'

'Some,' I hedged. I had after all read the *Times* or something on the way down here.

'I've got some press cuttings on Davidov,' said Proctor. 'I'll let you have them. You might find them revealing.'

'Thanks,' I said. 'But I still don't see what you want me to do.'

'Talk to the Pedersens,' he said. 'See if you can get them to give away anything about where the stamps are now.'

'Why should they tell me anything?'

'You have a natural talent,' said Proctor. 'Look at how much I've told you.'

'What's in it for me?' I asked.

'A thousand Pounds, if I recover the stamps.'

'Two thousand,' I said.

'OK,' he said. 'Done.'

Which was just a touch too easy. But I just said:

'OK.'

I'd obviously just been set up. Oh yes, I'd definitely been set up. Maybe in due course I would even discover what I'd been set up for. There was one way to find out.

It wasn't difficult tracking the Pedersens down. The hotel wasn't that big and there were not that many of us in it. Mrs Pedersen proved to be very talkative. Once she had started talking it was quite difficult to stop her, though I tried once or twice. During my stroll round the garden with her, I established a number of things. Roughly in order of importance to the case, these were:

1. Both she and her husband originally came from Nykø-bing, but they lived in a flat in Copenhagen when they were in Denmark, which at the moment they were not.

2. Her children were called Henning and Anna. Anna was named after her great aunt, who lived in Randers. You pronounced it 'Ran'ers'. Randers is nice, but not as nice as Nykøbing. Henning was not named after anyone in particular. They had thought of calling him Arne, but didn't.

3. Pedersen is one of the most common names in Denmark, though not as common as Andersen. You

pronounced it 'An'ersen.' Andersen was extremely common.

4. The public transport system in Copenhagen is one of the most efficient in the world.

5. It has to be efficient because the tax on cars is so high. Really, all taxes in Denmark are far too high.

6. The Swedes all drive cars that are much too big. Global warming is caused almost entirely by Swedes. (I think she said this last bit. I was beginning to glaze over by then.)

7. The good thing about flea markets was that the government has not, so far, found any way of taxing them.

8. But they will.

She also made various other points that were not so relevant to the case, but those were the main ones. I tried to grill her on the stamps, but she looked blank and told me a fascinating anecdote about her grandmother in Aalborg.

When I woke up, she had gone.

I reported this back to the weasel, who just nodded, as though this was what he had been expecting.

'If that was what you were expecting,' I said, 'then you were wasting my time—I'm assuming I collect my money only if we recover the stamps?'

'Yes,' he said, 'but I have not wasted my time.' He held up a key.

'I'm presumably supposed to ask you what that key is,' I said.

'In which case, I would tell you that it is a hotel pass key, that will let us into the Pedersens' room. Would you like to know how I got it?'

'Good for you,' I said, thinking of the last time I had let myself into somebody else's room at that hotel. 'But I regret to inform you that key does not involve me in the slightest. I just said I'd talk to them, which I have done.'

'But you discovered nothing.'

'OK, let's just call the deal off,' I said.

He handed me the small, cold, silvery object. 'I'll create a diversion,' he suggested, 'and you get into the room and take a look round.'

'No,' I said.

'Remember, there's two thousand in it for you.'

'I'll want three thousand if I'm to start breaking into rooms,' I said.

'OK,' he said. 'Done.'

Yes, I'd been set up. But set up for *what* exactly?

The weasel and I agreed he would divert the Pedersens with his scintillating conversation and, once he had tipped me the wink, I would sneak off and spend five minutes (no more) checking likely hiding places. I would then return the key to him, which he would replace in the room behind reception.

It was half an hour or so later that I saw him seated amongst the Pedersens, becoming an expert on Mrs Pedersen's aunts by marriage. I had spent some of that half hour reading the press cuttings on Grigory Davidov that Proctor had pushed under my door. They made an interesting study—I was forced to conclude that, apart from his affection for chocolate, he was not a nice man. That didn't make Herbie Proctor any less of a creep, of course, nor did it mean I trusted him any more than I had done. Looking at him, hanging eagerly onto Mrs Pedersen's every last word, it was clear that there could be little about him that was genuine.

Herbie winked at me. I winked back and headed off up the stairs.

But not to the Pedersens' room. Of course not. What precisely do you take me for? It was not just that it was a crap plan. It was the weasel's crap plan. So I hid round a corner, from where I could just see the Pedersens' door. And I waited.

I did not have to wait very long at all. Approximately two minutes into what should have been my search, I heard footsteps on the stairs. A small party came into view—one weasel and two Pedersens. Mrs Pedersen was walking on tiptoes and looking quite excited. Mr Pedersen wasn't. The weasel pointed to the room I was supposed to be in and sauntered off downstairs, looking unjustifiably pleased. Mrs Pedersen pushed her key into the lock and turned it, then flung the door open. She burst into what was (as various people were about to discover) a room containing no literary agents of any kind. Her husband followed sceptically.

After a short pause, both re-emerged, Mrs Pedersen looking puzzled and Mr Pedersen looking smug. It was not necessary to know the Danish for 'I told you so' in order to work out roughly what each of them had been expecting.

So, yes...I'd been set up... but why?

'I agree,' said Ethelred, 'that Proctor's behaviour was odd.'

I spluttered a bit at this understatement, but let Ethelred prattle on. A nugget of enlightenment might emerge out of the general dross, if I gave him long enough.

'Think about it though,' he said. 'The whole business of Proctor hiding something at the station is your word against his. If he *has* hidden something, then he urgently needs the police to believe him and not you. At the moment neither of you, frankly, have much credibility. On the other hand if you start interrogating innocent Danes and then try to burgle their room, it might make the police think, on the basis of probability, that you are the one with criminal intent and that you have been trying to incriminate Proctor. The pressure will be off him long enough for him to do whatever he needs to do.'

'So, we have proof, if that were needed, that Proctor *has* hidden something valuable in left luggage.'

'But what?' said Ethelred.

'Stamps?' I suggested.

'We may discount the entire stamp story,' said Ethelred. 'Who was that client again?'

'H C Andersen,' I said.

'I think that somebody has been telling you fairy stories,' said Ethelred. 'But let us at least check Mr Pedersen's credentials. I'm pretty sure I can get the number of the Danish Embassy from reception.'

He returned a couple of minutes later and dialled a number on his mobile.

'*Godmorgen. Jeg vil gerne taler med Herr Pedersen,*' he said in what may or may not have been fluent Danish. I'd forgotten that was one of Ethelred's less useful accomplishments.

There was a pause as Ethelred was told something.

'*Hvornar kommer Han igen?*'

Another pause as Ethelred was told other, possibly different, things.

'*Nej tak. Jeg vil ringer igen senere. Tusind tak.*'

He snapped his phone shut.

'Well?' I said. 'You're looking pretty smug, so spit it out before I have to do something unpleasant to take the smile off your face.'

'Proctor lied,' said Ethelred. 'He said there was nobody called Pedersen at the Embassy. Well, there's a Georg Pedersen in their commercial section. He's away at the moment, but he is due back tomorrow. Looks like the Pedersens are the real thing.'

'So, no doubt about it—Herbie set me up to look stupid?' I said.

'That would seem to be the case.'

'Well, I said, 'if that's the worst he can do...'

It was at that point that the police turned up and said that they had a few more questions to ask me.

CHAPTER 21

So, I was back in the little office just off Reception. It seemed smaller and even less tidy. There were more dirty cups. There were more dirty plates. Somebody had left a slice of cold pizza on top of a file. Otherwise it was all much as before.

The Inspector lit a *Gauloise*, showing that, if there was anti-smoking legislation in France, it did not apply to the police.

'I thought we had an agreement that I was not under arrest, so long as I didn't attack policemen,' I pointed out.

'You are not under arrest, but there are new facts to consider,' he said.

'But I *haven't done anything*,' I said.

The Inspector raised his eyebrows. He had possibly heard that one before.

'OK,' I said, 'I have broken into the scene of a crime, eaten key evidence, left the hotel suspiciously and jumped on a policeman from the top of the garden wall. But otherwise, I *haven't done anything.*'

His eyebrows had not returned to their normal position (unless raised was their normal position, of course).

'What?' I said.

'*Monsieur* Davidov was poisoned,' he said.

'Yes,' I said. 'We know that—cyanide in the peach truffle. Not nice but, equally, not me.'

'The chocolates were from Apollinaire.'

'Obviously,' I said.

'You purchased chocolates from Apollinaire,' he said.

I decided not to say 'obviously' again. I could see this might be leading somewhere.

'Half the guests in the hotel must have bought chocolates there,' I said.

'The shop assistant remembers only you and *Monsieur* Davidov.'

'That's possible. True connoisseurs of the chocolatier's art are rare.'

'She remembers you going on about the peach truffles.'

'And the orange creams and the ganaches,' I said. 'Look, I don't know about the poisoning.'

'So you have said. Let us turn, however, to *Monsieur* Davidov. Did you know him well?'

This was much easier. 'I had never heard of him until I arrived here,' I said.

'Never?'

'Absolutely.'

'Then why,' said the Inspector, 'had you made this collection of press cuttings about him?'

He held up the folder that Herbie Proctor had kindly pushed under my door.

'Hang on one minute!' I said. 'Proctor gave me those.'

'It was definitely *Monsieur* Proctor?'

'Without a doubt.'

'And when was this?' he asked.

'He pushed them under my door earlier today—or somebody did anyway. You see…'

'Somebody? So—let me get this straight—you are not certain it was *Monsieur* Proctor? You now say that the cuttings were in fact pushed under your door by an unknown person?'

'Yes. But obviously the unknown person *was* Herbie Proctor.'

' "Obviously" in what sense? Did you see him?'

'No, the folder just appeared. But it must have been him...'
I was desperately trying to remember exactly what Proctor had
said about the cuttings.

'You had an argument with *Monsieur* Gold?' asked the
Inspector.

'Sort of...' I hedged. Was I about to be accused of two
murders?

'You disliked him?'

'No,' I said, quickly correcting any erroneous impression on
this score. 'Actually, I really, really liked him.'

'You were good friends?'

'Very,' I said. Well, we would have been, given another night
in the hotel.

The Inspector frowned. 'We had long suspected that *Monsieur*
Gold and his environmentalist colleagues had some intention of
harming *Monsieur* Davidov. Had Gold not been killed, we think
that he might have made such an attempt. Your close friendship,
as you describe it, with *Monsieur* Gold suggests perhaps that you
might have been working together?'

OK, that was the wrong answer then. What I should have
said was that I scarcely knew Jonathan Gold. Was it too late to
point out that I made him puke?

'Let me explain,' I said, though it did seem to me that explanations had largely got me where I was now, and that perhaps
shutting up might be a good plan.

The Inspector in any case waved a hand dismissively.

'Let me suggest to you, *Mademoiselle* Thirkettle, that what
actually happened was this. For a long time you have interested
yourself in *Monsieur* Davidov's career. No?'

'No,' I said.

'You gathered together this...' He waved his hand at the
heap of paper. '... collection of press cuttings, mainly from the

left-wing papers. You came to this hotel, you say, to meet your friend *Monsieur* Tressider. But in fact it was to assassinate *Monsieur* Davidov. You met up with the accomplice, Jonathan Gold. To throw people off the scent, he pretended to find you ugly and repulsive.'

'Not *that* ugly and repulsive,' I said. 'Actually, I think, given the proper atmosphere, with soft lights and the right sort of chocolate...'

The Inspector again waved a dismissive hand.

'Exactly. We come to the question of the chocolate. You purchased truffles knowing that Grigory Davidov's favourite was peach. You injected cyanide, obtained from an unknown source—but perhaps given to you by *Monsieur* Gold, who we believe utilised poisons as part of his profession—into the very truffle he would certainly choose first. You thought that, by pretending to a quite unbelievable ignorance of current affairs, you would escape suspicion. Later, however, you could not resist returning to the scene of the crime and removing the only evidence that would have linked you incontrovertibly with the murder. Later still, you tried to escape over the wall, perhaps to dispose of the container in which you had brought the cyanide; but having been spotted by *Monsieur* Proctor, who had suspected you of criminal intent, you were obliged to return.'

I shut my mouth, which for some reason had fallen open during the course of this account of my actions. I thought for a moment. Then I opened my mouth again.

'That's crap, that is,' I pointed out.

'Is it?'

'I can prove it!' I said. 'Fingerprint those cuttings. They'll have the weasel's dabs all over them.'

'The weasel?'

'Herbie Proctor.'

'*Monsieur* Proctor has told us,' said the Inspector, 'that you made him read the cuttings last night. He had no real interest, but he dutifully looked at each of them, he said. Every single one.'

Well, at least I now knew roughly what I'd been set up for.

'I'll kill that slimy little scumbag,' I said. 'Just tell me where I can lay my hands on some strychnine and then let me out of this room for five minutes. I promise I'll be back here later to answer any other questions, but right now I need a bit of quality time with Herbie Proctor.'

'You are planning a further murder perhaps?' asked the Inspector.

'Just let me kill Proctor,' I said, 'and I'll confess to any two other murders of your choice.'

'The offer is certainly tempting,' said the Inspector. 'But it would not really help matters. Do you know why *Monsieur* Proctor would wish to frame you?'

Let's see…he was a scumbag, I had spurned his obnoxious advances, I'd managed to have his stomach pumped, I'd tricked him into ordering a ruinously expensive lunch. None of that quite seemed enough. I pointed this out.

'That is what we thought too,' said the Inspector. 'But he does seem very keen to implicate you for some reason. I think *Monsieur* Proctor is not being entirely truthful. Nor is he quite as clever as he imagines.'

'And you think I am being truthful?'

'You behaviour has been very odd—your clumsy investigations, your even clumsier attempt to get back into the hotel you had got out of, your amazing ignorance of current affairs. But *Monsieur* Tressider says that you read only the *Bookseller* and *Hello! Magazine*?'

'And the book reviews,' I said. 'I read *all* the book reviews.'

The Inspector nodded.

'It seemed to us that you were either being very, very clever or rather stupid.'

'Well, perhaps I am being very, very clever,' I suggested.

He shook his head. 'No, we ruled that out some time ago.'

'Thanks a bunch,' I said. 'So is that it?'

'Not quite. If *Monsieur* Proctor did push the cuttings under your door—and it was *Monsieur* Proctor who suggested we should search your room while you were otherwise engaged—then to what end? It also means that *Monsieur* Proctor has been collecting cuttings about Grigory Davidov for some time. Why should that be, I wonder?'

'He claims to be a private detective,' I said. 'He claims to have come here looking for those Danish stamps. His client is a Mr H C...well, he's a Danish bloke. He wants his stamps back.'

'But that is clearly not the real reason,' said the Inspector. 'The story about the stamps is an inept attempt to throw somebody off the scent. Perhaps he is trying to throw you off the scent, but more likely he is hoping ultimately to fool me. We have good reason to believe that his presence here too was linked in some way to Grigory Davidov's stay. Gold, Davidov and Proctor seem to share a past. The question is: why was Davidov here?'

'To buy stamps?'

'Yes, he does seem to have been a genuine stamp collector. As I said, however, there have been a lot of threats against him. He usually travels with his own bodyguards—what do you call them? *Les personnes aux crânes rasés.* Do you still say 'skinheads'? But they were not with him this time. Whatever he was doing here was something that he was not keen anyone should know about—even his own people. I do not believe that he came to buy stamps. He seems to have been quite embarrassed about his real reason for being here. And *Monsieur* Davidov was not a man who was embarrassed easily, I think.'

'But Herbie Proctor knows the reason?'

'Perhaps. If he was the person who slipped the press cuttings under the door. *Monsieur* Proctor claims however that the cuttings are not his. Could it have been somebody else?'

'Herbie Boy lied about my forcing him to read them. That being the case, there would seem to be only one way his fingerprints could get on the press cuttings.'

The Inspector nodded. 'He is trying to divert my attention from something.'

'What?' I asked.

'If I knew that,' he said with a smile, 'I suspect I would know all I needed to know, but as it is...'

He shrugged. Shrugging was spreading in Chaubord like athlete's foot in a school with one towel.

I went to the bar, hoping to find coffee and possibly snacks containing detectable traces of chocolate. There was no sign of either. I was about to leave again when I noticed that the doorway through which I had planned to pass was occupied by a Danish child carrying a magnifying glass.

'Hi, kid,' I said in a friendly manner.

In return he looked at me through the magnifying glass, probably making me appear size 120 (British) approx.

'They arrested you,' he said.

'It's called Helping the Police with their Enquiries,' I said.

'You don't look as though you'd be that much help,' he said.

'Appearances,' I said haughtily, 'can be deceptive. What's it to you, anyway?'

He had put down the glass and taken out a small notebook.

'I would like you to answer some questions,' said the annoying child.

'Clear off,' I said. 'I'm not your mother.'

He made a note of this in his book.

'Question one,' he continued. 'Did you murder Mr Davidov?'

'No,' I said.

The annoying child noted this too.

'Question two: did you murder Mr Gold?'

'No,' I said.

Another note in the book.

'Question three: do you know who did?'

'Herbie Proctor,' I said.

The annoying child flicked back through his notebook, which (I noticed) already seemed quite full.

'He says that *you* did,' he said.

'It's an old trick,' I pointed out. 'Shift the blame onto some innocent party.'

'Is it?'

'Trust me.'

He noted this.

'Question four,' continued the child. 'Did you see anything suspicious?'

'When?' I asked.

The child consulted his notebook. 'It doesn't say,' he said.

'I saw Grigory Davidov talking to Jonathan Gold,' I said.

'Was either of them killing the other one?'

'Not at the time.'

The annoying child did not consider this worth noting.

'Question five,' he said. 'Do you have any knives or poison with you?'

This was clearly designed to catch me unawares.

'Just the two large knives and a bottle of strychnine,' I said.

'It wasn't strychnine,' he said. 'It's too slow.'

So, he did know a bit about detective work, then.

'I would seem to be in the clear in that case,' I said.

'Yes, but you should not leave the hotel,' he said. 'I may need to question you again. Oh, and if my sister asks you any questions, by the way, do not tell her anything. She is not a real detective.'

CHAPTER 22

When you are booking a holiday, the idea of staying in a small hotel seems quite attractive. Why pay for things like an indoor swimming pool and gym that you will probably never use? Why have a television with thirty channels, when you will only watch one? Who really wants a bewildering array of international breakfast items first thing in the morning? If Germans and Norwegians want cheese for breakfast, good luck to them, but a choice of bacon or kippers is good enough for normal people. All you need, after all, is a comfortable bed, a simple but nourishing breakfast and a good location close to whatever museums, beaches or bars you plan to visit. The sort of luxury provided by large five star establishments is a complete waste of money.

As your second day of captivity in a small hotel wears on however, it does occur to you that a little five star luxury would not go amiss. On day one, the fact that the television in your room provides only the local channels seems quaint and charming. On day two that news story about foot and mouth in the Auvergne is beginning to lose its initial interest. On day two you realise that you may as well linger over breakfast, because there isn't much else to do. On day two you think you really might like to spend an hour on the rowing machine.

It was during the bleak, empty hour after lunch that I ran into Georg Pedersen. I had spoken to him briefly shortly after we had both arrived, when the hotel was still full of stamp collectors. He seemed to be taking his incarceration better than most of the other guests. He was wearing an expensive looking cashmere jacket with well-cut jeans and a soft cotton shirt—a slightly less formal version of what he wore daily at the Embassy. His dark hair was cut short. His countenance was completely untroubled.

'It's a bad business,' he said. 'Have you heard whether the police are close to finding the killer?'

'Your guess is as good as mine,' I said.

'I suppose,' he continued, 'the surprise is that nobody managed to kill Davidov sooner. He has plenty of enemies out there. Some hate him because he has made a lot of money and nobody can quite tell how. The more perceptive hate him as a symbol of capitalism at its worst—the sort of capitalism that sucks the blood out of a community and then moves on. Yacoubabad hangs over him, even if nothing was ever proved. Then there is what his oil company has got up to in Nigeria.'

'You seem to know a lot about him,' I said.

'It's my job,' he said. 'I have to understand these things.'

'What do you do at the Embassy?' I asked.

'I am in the commercial section,' he said.

That seemed to be all the explanation I was getting. It struck me that Pedersen might have a more shadowy role, or that, equally, he might just be a First Secretary Commercial with a passing interest in the environment.

'I would have thought,' I said to him, 'that you could have claimed diplomatic immunity and avoided all this?'

'Perhaps,' he said. 'I have phoned my Ambassador, and he is anxious that we are seen to help the police with their enquiries. He did ask me whether I had in fact murdered either of the gentlemen in question, but happily I was able to tell him that I had not. Given that assurance, he felt that it was better that we stayed. We are in any case still waiting for our heavy baggage to arrive from Moscow, so we are as comfortable here as we would be at our flat in Paris.'

'You're originally from Nykøbing?' I said.

'Yes,' he said. 'Both my wife and I. We travelled back from Moscow via Denmark, so we visited our respective families there last weekend. Jutland is pretty bleak in the winter, though. Fortunately it is not as bleak as Russia.'

'Did you talk much to Davidov?' I asked.

'Once or twice. And you?'

'Once or twice,' I said. 'I spoke to both him and Gold.'

'Ah, yes, Gold,' said Pedersen. 'Why was he here, do you think? He was not a stamp collector.'

'No,' I said.

'People do come to the Loire in the winter. Mr Gold may have just wanted to visit the chateaux off-season when there were fewer people around. He did of course have links with environmental groups. He had spoken at a number of conferences in Europe. He had strong views as to what should happen to people like Davidov.'

'You know that?'

'Yes, I know that. It is part of my job.'

'In the Commercial Section?'

'Oh yes, certainly—in the Commercial Section,' he said.

Pedersen's comments about Gold's links with environmental groups were interesting, though they only confirmed things that had been said during one conversation that I had had with Gold. It was not conclusive but it added to a picture that was already developing in my mind. I was beginning to think that I knew who had killed Gold and (though, on the face of it, it seemed impossible) who had killed Davidov. It wasn't a matter of new evidence—just of having gone round the track so many times that I had ruled out everything else. If I was right, then I could be reasonably certain nobody was coming after me.

Anyway, I had my own problem to solve. If my contact was Gold or Davidov, then (as I've said) that was that. But what if it was Brown? In that sense, Elsie's discovery that his stay at the hotel had been long planned was interesting. I couldn't quite believe that it was Proctor, but the mysterious object he had hidden could well be the mysterious object that formed part of my instructions. Taylor had had plenty of opportunities to make himself known to me and had done nothing. Jones was the one I knew least well. I decided to seek him out.

Like most of the guests, Jones led a peripatetic life, migrating, as one room become intolerably boring, to another that was briefly more interesting. I found him sitting out on the terrace, bundled up in an overcoat and scarf. The overcoat looked as if it might have been expensive when it had been bought ten or fifteen years before. It was well cut, but (even to my eye) slightly old fashioned. The colourful new scarf, possibly purchased expressly to brighten it up, made the coat seem even more faded. At the same time, the well-cut coat made the red scarf look cheap. It was fortunate that he had decided not to wear a hat. Jones had either not shaved that morning or had shaved badly with an old razor. Grey stubble appeared patchily across his chin and up one cheek. He looked unhappy.

'So,' I said, taking the chair beside him, 'we're still stuck here.'

This made him even unhappier. 'And who's paying?' he asked. 'That's what I want to know.'

'The police are paying for the hotel,' I said, 'as long as we have to stay here.'

'I know that, but where's my ticket home?' he said. 'I had a booking on a train the day before yesterday. That ticket's no good now. I'm going to have to buy another one. Who'll pay for it, eh?'

I made what I thought was a sympathetic smile.

'You can laugh, but it's not funny,' he said. 'You're probably working, aren't you?'

I had not done any actual writing for months but I nodded. Writers are used to deluding themselves that all sorts of things are 'work'—searching the Internet for references to themselves, checking their Amazon ranking, blogging, making coffee. I'd done a few of those. I was working.

'There you are,' he said. 'I don't even have my pension now.'

I decided I had better ask why, even though I suspected I might be in for a long explanation. I was. It was an unhappy story, but not uncommon these days. He had worked all his life for the same company, making parts for motorcars. He had dutifully paid into a company pension scheme, and had, year after year, watched his older colleagues go off to a comfortable retirement. There are few good reasons for working in much the same job for forty years, day in, day out; but as Jones got older himself, the pension scheme had seemed a reasonably sound reason. He too would retire, early if possible, and enjoy a comfortable old age. Then, when he was sixty-four, the company had folded. A foreign firm had stepped in to rescue the operation, but not to shore up the pension scheme. It was too late to go anywhere else or do anything else. You could say his bitterness was not unreasonable. I raised my eyebrows when he told me the name of the company. He seemed unaware of the coincidence. Or perhaps, having let it slip, he didn't wish to draw my attention to it.

'So, have you bought any stamps?' I asked. 'Or were you here on any other business?'

'Other business?' he asked, puzzled.

We looked at each other. There was no conspiratorial wink, no hint of recognition.

'OK, I just wondered,' I said.

'What other business could I have?' he asked.

'None, I guess,' I said lamely.

Well, I'd given him a chance to reveal himself if he was my contact. Either he was playing it very cool or he was a stamp collector who had probably begun to think I was slightly odd in the head. I mentally chalked up a cross against his name and wondered how quickly I could escape. There was, I knew from past experience at the hotel, a danger he would start talking about stamps and not stop. Ever.

'No, I was just buying stamps,' he said. 'Actually, I looked, mainly. No money now, you see. I just bought one or two. I collect European stamps—German, Norwegian, Swedish, Danish, Finnish and so on.'

'But not the ten kroner puce, eh?' I said with a smile. It was a good line to sign off on. He was supposed to chuckle. I was supposed to stand allowing me and my sanity to make a graceful exit.

He did not chuckle. 'Yes. I wish I'd been at that flea market. Whoever bought the stamps probably had no idea what they'd got hold of.'

'I bet they do now, though,' I said. I stood up anyway.

'I'm sure they do. And they'll probably keep quiet about it. The only people who'll make money out of the affair in the end will be the lawyers.'

'True,' I said. 'I suspect it will all end up in court.'

'Probably,' he said. 'Still, it would be good to have one of those stamps as my pension fund. Do you know by the way what was the most expensive item sold at a stamp auction?'

I guessed we all knew that. I sank back into my chair. I wondered if I got the answer right whether I could still escape. 'The Swedish three skilling yellow,' I said.

He smiled sadly and shook his head. 'Not by a long way. That went for a mere two point eight seven million Swiss Francs. A cover bearing both the one penny and two penny Mauritius

'Post Office' stamps sold for five point seven five million. Five point seven. Plenty of people think it's the treskilling yellow, but they're way out.'

'I'll do my best to remember that,' I said, trying to stifle a yawn.

Then I got lucky. Without warning, Jones got to his feet. 'God, I hate being cooped up here,' he exclaimed suddenly. 'I hate being cooped up anywhere. I just hope they let us go today.'

I agreed that would be good, and watched him march off abruptly into the hotel. Perhaps his swift departure had had to do with nothing except the cold out there on the terrace.

He had of course just revealed a perfectly sound reason for disliking Davidov—maybe sound enough for a murder. But, as I say, I did not really suspect him of murder. And the strangest coincidences often have the simplest explanations.

CHAPTER 23

Sod all (pardon my French) seemed to have changed at the Vieille Auberge since it had been built a hundred and fifty years ago, when France had still had an Emperor in Paris and a number of kings in exile. There is, as my old dad always used to say, no substitute for quality, and the fake beams would have looked as crap then as they did now. The architect had clearly been a fan of the Middle Ages, and had successfully incorporated into his design most of the worst aspects of fourteenth century life. Between meals there was not much to do except sit in the gloom and wait patiently for the Black Death.

In reception, tucked away as far as was possible, sat the one concession to the twenty first century—a single computer with American software and a French keyboard. I sat down with the intention of checking my emails, and then another thought occurred to me. It was time to check out Davidov a little more thoroughly. I located Google, typed 'Grigory Davidov' and hit the return key.

I found myself (Google informed me) on page 1 of about 395,000. Google told me that this had taken it 0.23 seconds (smug git). There was plenty on Davidov out there—including a lot about his career to date and his ambitions for the future. There was much speculation that his money had initially been made in activity that was more or less criminal. He had links with the Mafia. The Russian authorities were belatedly investigating him—hence perhaps his recently announced desire to move the centre of his operations to London. He had acquired a house near Holland Park but had not yet moved into it. He had expressed his admiration for a number of football teams that he had hoped to buy. I drifted from site to site as one does, ending up in YouTube, where I had been directed to a video of Davidov speaking to a group of businessmen at some fund-raising event. This led to another video of Davidov leaving a hotel, being barracked by some nice young people who held placards bearing the word 'Yacoubabad'.

So, there it was. He mixed with criminals but, since he was a bit of a criminal himself, this was not very surprising. Similarly it was not surprising that people who were generally in favour of the environment did not like him. The second video was coming to an end, and I was just about to log out when something about the footage struck me as odd. So I replayed it.

Then I replayed it another ten times.

At first, as you watched the video run through, there wasn't much to go on. This was not professional footage by any standards. Davidov is seen leaving an anonymous hotel. The quality of the picture was lousy, as if captured on a mobile phone or a very cheap camera held by somebody who had no idea what they were doing. Davidov looks this way and that, trying to work out how to get through the crowd. People shout things at him in German, because that is the country he seems to be in. There is also a voice saying something in English, but you can't quite make out what. Goo-stone mounds? Ghost time mines? Something of the sort. Only as Davidov pushes forward, does the often-repeated phrase become more or less understandable.

'What about the Goldstein diamonds?' somebody calls.

Davidov stops dead, frowns and looks into the crowd, searching for something. Then he presses on, almost against his will, propelled by one or two of his people, who have suddenly appeared. The camera pans back across the crowd of protestors.

Towards the back I catch a quick glimpse of a familiar face. On the sixth or seventh viewing I am certain. It is Jonathan Gold. Each time, he smiles at the camera for an instant and then turns away. But, each and every time, it is Jonathan Gold all right.

There was only one way of following this up. I went back to Google and typed in, with no small amount of interest, 'Goldstein diamonds'.

I was planning to find Ethelred and tell him what I had discovered, but I found my way barred by a Danish child.

'Your brother says you're not a detective,' I said. 'And in any case, I'm not answering any more stupid questions today. Clear off.'

Her lower lip started to tremble. A tear began to well up in her eye. She was building up for a massive, heart-rending sob. This made me feel sort of uncomfortable. I suddenly realised that this was, perhaps, what guilt felt like.

'OK, OK, just make it snappy,' I said.

'That was my intention anyway,' she said, taking out a sheet of paper and a pencil. 'Shall we begin?'

So, some advice for you: never trust small blonde girls with large, tearful blue eyes. Don't trust any of them. Got that? OK then…

'OK, then,' I said. 'What do you want to know? Would you like me to tell you who killed Mr Davidov?'

'No,' she said. 'I think my daddy already knows that.'

'Does he now? I thought he was in the commercial section of the Danish Embassy, not a detective.'

'He has to say that's what he does,' said the girl.

'And what is he really?'

'Promise you won't tell anyone?'

'Absolutely,' I said.

'OK. He really works for the *Forsvarets Efterretningstjeneste*,' she said.

That obviously made things a lot clearer.

'What?' I said.

She repeated it.

'I'll take your word for it,' I said.

'He's a spy,' she said, 'but nobody is supposed to know.'

A bit more advice. If you are a spy and are reading this, don't tell any blonde haired girls with large, tearful blue eyes. Got that? OK, then...

'So why is he here?'

'I think to watch the fat man.' She frowned with concentration. 'I wanted to go to Disneyland.'

'Right,' I said. 'But your father doesn't actually kill people, eh?'

'No,' said the blonde girl. 'It was my brother. I'm going to send this to the police.'

She handed me the piece of paper. It read: 'My brother Henning killed the fat Russian man and nice Jonathan. Please arrest him now.'

'But,' I said, 'isn't your brother going to be annoyed when they arrest him? He's obviously being framed.'

'Yes, but he won't know it's me,' she said. 'The note is anonymous. I haven't signed it.' She pointed to the blank space at the end.

'Good point,' I said. 'But I still wouldn't do it.'

'Why?'

'Because the real murderer,' I said confidentially, 'is a man called Herbie Proctor.'

She looked at me contemptuously.

'And you really believe that?' she said.

I thought of saying, 'yes'—but then I didn't. Small blonde girls can be very scathing.

OK, off to tell Ethelred about the Internet, then.

CHAPTER 24

Elsie appeared worryingly pleased with herself. I knew that look and how often it had, in the past, spelt trouble, though not usually for her.

I had been sitting peacefully in the garden, enjoying the afternoon sun. I would have been quite happy to stay there undisturbed, but Elsie had stuff she needed to tell somebody.

'There's this thing called the "Internet",' she began.

'Yes,' I said. 'I've come across it. You *don't* need to do that thing with your fingers to show the word is in inverted commas. Disapproval of one or two aspects of the twenty-first century and a complete ignorance of modern technology are not the same. Just because I don't wear a hoodie and my underpants don't show above my trousers, it does not follow I am unacquainted with the Internet.'

'If you say so,' she said. 'I do have to point out however that you wear brown brogues with industrial strength soles. You wear checked flannel shirts in the summer. All your jackets are made of tweed, except for the linen ones. I am not in a position to comment on your underpants, but let's just say I have my suspicions.'

'Nevertheless, I do know what the Internet is.'

'OK—now on the "Internet", is this thing called "YouTube". Don't pretend to have heard of it.'

'It has videos on it. And stop doing that thing with your fingers.'

'A good guess,' said Elsie with a patronising nod. 'Yes, it has videos posted by random people. There were some of Davidov. There was one of him making a speech and there was one of him being heckled by people—some of them wore gorilla masks, though I'm not sure why.'

'And your point is?' I asked.

'The pictures looked as though they had been taken by somebody on their "mobile phone".'

I looked at her pointedly.

'OK, I'll stop doing that thing with my fingers,' she conceded with some reluctance. 'The point is that one of the hecklers was Jonathan Gold. He kept calling out: what about the Goldstein Diamonds? Davidov looked really worried.'

'That's interesting,' I said. 'I'd be worried if I had them.'

'You know about them?'

'A bit,' I said. 'They are famously unlucky jewels.'

I explained to Elsie what I knew—I'd taken an interest in the story because it had seemed to me that it might contain the plot for a future novel. Even as I retold it, it struck me that it contained a nice combination of irony and hubris. Back in 1914, the Czar had commissioned what was to be the finest necklace ever made. A St Petersburg jeweller began a search for the highest quality gems from all over the world. The outbreak of war in August that year made his task more challenging, but throughout 1915 and 1916 he was still designing, buying, assembling. By March 1917 it was complete. Legend has it that he arrived at the Winter Palace with the jewels and his invoice just as it was being stormed by the communists—but that would mean he delayed invoicing for six months. What seems to have happened in fact is that between the February and October Revolutions he pressed the various administrations for payment. Strangely none of them thought it was a priority. It was inevitable that after the Bolsheviks came to power he would be arrested. He was shot some time in 1918. He was the first victim of what became known as the unluckiest necklace in the world. Somebody smuggled it out of Russia and in the 20s and 30s it was owned by a succession of rich Americans. One, an actress, had a bad fall while filming on the United Artists lot and never worked again. A stock-broker bought it for his wife in 1929, and jumped from his office window twenty storeys above Wall Street a month later. It travelled back across the Atlantic when it was sold to a German banker named Goldstein in 1935. He lost it when he fled Germany after Hitler came to power. The necklace finally vanished around the end of the war. It was believed to have gone home to Russia, but nobody knew for sure. Then, out of the blue, Davidov's wife appeared in public wearing something that seemed to be the Goldstein diamonds. There's just one blurry photograph, which Davidov quickly claimed was costume jewellery modelled on an old Russian design. The necklace, whatever it was, never reappeared. It was just after that that the disaster at Yacoubabad occurred and only a little later that Davidov lost one of his key political contacts and the investigation into his activities began.

'So,' I concluded, 'Maybe Davidov has them or had them—who knows? There is of course another theory that they ended up in the pocket of some lucky GI, who chanced on them as the Allies advanced eastwards, and that they are at the bottom of a drawer in Milwaukee WI or Boulder Creek CA.'

Elsie looked slightly miffed. She obviously resented the fact that I had heard of her diamonds.

'There's a lot about them in the "newspapers",' I said.

'Stop doing that thing with your fingers,' she said. 'It's really irritating. Anyway, there have been one or two stories in the papers lately saying that if Davidov had the diamonds it pretty much proved his links with the Russian underworld and he would not be permitted to join the Manchester United Supporters' Club, let alone buy shares.'

'I know,' I said.

Elsie's look indicated that I knew too much for my own good. 'Sorry,' I said.

'So,' Elsie said, either accepting or ignoring my apology, 'Gold knew something about the diamonds.'

'*Everybody* except you knew about the diamonds, Elsie.'

'Davidov looked dead worried though,' mused Elsie. 'I'd say Davidov had still got the diamonds, and Gold had proof.'

'All that? On the basis of a fuzzy twenty second clip on YouTube?'

'Yup,' said Elsie. However wrong Elsie's last snap judgment may have been, it rarely makes her doubt the next one.

'In which case,' I said, 'Gold would have been in a position to end Davidov's hopes of buying a major club.'

'The plot thickens,' said Elsie. 'If Gold was trying to blackmail Davidov, that would be a powerful motive. Davidov seems to have had other people murdered for standing in his way.'

'But nobody has suggested he carried out any killings personally,' I said.

'But Davidov could have thought it worth paying Gold off?'

'In which case,' I said, 'the thing that was in Davidov's white envelope might have been cash to shut Gold up?'

'You heard them arguing,' said Elsie. 'What did they say?'

What indeed? There they had been in the small, stuffy sitting room. Gold had his fist raised. Davidov was laughing. 'That's not going to help get them back,' Davidov had said. 'You really don't understand what I could do to you, do you?' Gold had replied. I had assumed that it was a physical threat that Gold was making. But of course—there were other types of threat. Then they saw me. We had had a brief conversation about Russian superstitions. Davidov had made his joke about things that were unlucky for him being unlucky for others too. Gold had scowled. I departed. But thinking back, yes, I was sure that Gold had been quite agitated, Davidov relatively calm. Weren't blackmailers supposed to show an icy detachment? My fictional ones always did. They rarely needed to shake their fists. That's the problem with real life crime: people don't know how to do it properly.

'What did they say?' asked Elsie.

'They stopped speaking as soon as I came into the room,' I said.

'Didn't you listen at the door first?'

'No.'

She snorted derisively.

'No,' I said. 'I don't listen at doors.'

'Everybody listens at doors.'

'No they don't.'

Elsie was prepared to consider this idea briefly before dismissing it as fantasy. She looked at me pityingly.

'Anyway,' I said, 'I've also discovered something interesting. Jones worked for a company taken over by DGE.'

Elsie looked blank.

'Davidov Global Enterprises,' I said. 'They took over the firm he worked for and then defaulted on the company pension scheme, leaving Jones pretty much penniless.'

'And Jones would have held him responsible?'

'I'm not sure he even connected DGE and Davidov,' I said. 'So many firms just go by their initials these days...'

'That's the problem—the hotel is full of people with only half a motive,' said Elsie. 'Maybe we should go back to the idea that somebody broke into the hotel?'

'The hotel was locked and the receptionist swears nobody came or went that night. As we know, the receptionist was, unusually, the only staff member in the hotel until the kitchen staff arrived in the morning. There's no evidence of a break-in— no sign of a locked window having been forced. Therefore it was somebody already in the hotel,' I said.

'What about the receptionist then?' Elsie asked.

I shook my head. 'A married man with children. No evidence he ever met Davidov or Gold before. He was expecting the manager to return to the hotel that night, so it isn't even the case that he knew in advance that his comings and goings would not be noticed. By the time the manager phoned him to say that he wouldn't be back until morning, Gold was probably already dead. Up to that point the receptionist was expecting his boss to walk through the door at any moment.'

'We are sure the manager couldn't have sneaked back unnoticed?' asked Elsie.

'He and his wife were staying with friends. There were apparently others at the dinner that night, so he has no shortage of witnesses.'

'What about the live-out staff?'

'They would have found it easier to get into the hotel, but the receptionist says he would have seen them if they had made their way upstairs to the guests' rooms.'

'So it has to be a guest?'

'Probably,' I said.

'I still don't know which,' said Elsie. 'Though I would like it to be Herbie Proctor. We know he has some links with Davidov.'

'I don't think so,' I said.

'The police do think so,' said Elsie. 'Why were you so keen to talk to Davidov anyway?'

'Was I?' I said.

'Yes, immediately after Gold's murder.'

'Oh, research—I just thought I might introduce some sociopolitical comment into my next book. Rankin does that sort of thing all the time.'

'That's different. Rankin's a highly respected prize winning author,' said Elsie.

'I almost won a prize once,' I said.

'A long time ago,' said Elsie.

'Yes, a long time ago,' I said.

'Pedersen wanted to talk to Davidov too apparently.'

'Really?'

'Pedersen is actually working for the Danish secret service. At last, according to his daughter—though she did, now I think of it, swear me to secrecy.'

'The *Forsvarets Efterretningstjeneste*?' I enquired.

'If you say so,' said Elsie.

'It doesn't surprise me,' I said. 'It would certainly explain why he might have been interested in Davidov. It doesn't mean that he killed him, though. It just means it's easier to understand what he was doing here. Of course his daughter could be making it up.'

'It still gets us no closer to knowing who committed either murder,' Elsie continued. 'Jones has a motive, but probably doesn't know it; Taylor's too wet; Brown has no apparent connection with anyone; the Danish family seem above-board. Bingo! It has to be Proctor.'

'It would help,' I said, 'to know what Proctor had deposited at left luggage.'

'I'm not risking a nocturnal foray again,' said Elsie with feeling.

'Have you noticed something, though?' I said.

She looked round the garden. 'There's nothing there to notice,' she said.

'That's the point,' I said.

'Stop being a dickhead, Tressider,' said Elsie, 'or I'll knee you in the groin. What are you talking about?'

I edged away and said: 'Just use your eyes, Elsie. There's no policeman.'

'Why?'

'I guess they've relaxed security,' I said. 'But I'm not sure why.'

We both looked round the garden. Nothing stirred.

'So, it's over the wall then?' she said.

'Let's try the gate,' I said. There was something fishy about this.

We walked over to the gate, until now firmly locked, even in my early pre-murder days at the hotel. I twisted the handle and it swung silently open.

'A bit too easy?' I asked.

'Let's go anyway,' said Elsie.

We slipped through the gate...

(HAPTER 25

···and out into the street.

'Oh shit! We still need the key!' The possessor of a large male brain stopped suddenly in his tracks.

'Yes,' I said. 'What a shame we didn't think of that before. Still, maybe I can find you one.'

'You know where it is?'

'I do,' I said.

My certainty may surprise you, but my reasoning was as follows. During the few moments that he had been out of my sight, Herbie boy had hidden the key somewhere that nobody could easily find it, but from where he could retrieve it quickly. The police had established that it was neither on nor (alas) inside his person. So, if he ever had it, he must have disposed of it rapidly right there in the lane. To be quite honest, the lane was composed of just three things:

1. Wall
2. Lane
3. Dog shit

He could not have dug up the tarmac so that left:

1. Wall

3. Dog shit

I thought I'd probably check the wall out first. I examined it carefully. It was another one of those examples of old-time crafts-manship that my father always used to go on about—frankly it was a miracle in fact that it was still standing. The pointing had long since parted company with the brickwork, leaving plentiful vertical and horizontal crevices of varying depth. I squatted down to see if I could see any glint of silver deep in any of the joints. At first there was nothing to catch the eye, then I noticed that a joint lower down was inexplicably and rather improbably stuffed up with dirt. Silly boy, Herbie. I took out my room key and scratched away for a bit. Almost immediately metal struck metal and I was able to extract a small device for opening lockers, with a round tag bearing the number '045'.

I held the key aloft in triumph.

'Is that it?' asked Ethelred.

'No,' I said, 'it's a completely different left luggage locker key. The wall is full of them. Why don't you see how many you can find?'

Ethelred looked at it. 'You realise he could never have swal-lowed it with that tag attached?' he asked.

I was about to argue that stranger things had happened when Ethelred said: 'Well done, but I think we should get moving before the police notice we are missing.'

This seemed as good a plan as any. We got moving.

In daylight the railway station looked kinder and friend-lier. It was one of those rather functional fifties buildings—lots of concrete, but quite homely with its green tiled roof, white walls and small casement windows. We felt conspicuous as we crossed the open space in front of it and even more conspic-uous as we entered the left luggage room. The room was lined with steel cabinets of two different sizes, all numbered and most with their keys still in the locks. To each key there was attached a disk of a perfectly swallow-able size. Apart from us, the room was deserted. There was a desk in one corner, belonging presumably to the guardian of this self-service facility, but it was unoccupied. It was not exactly high-security, but it probably did not need to be. We counted along the row of smaller lockers until we got to '045'. We put the key into the lock and turned it.

At first I thought that the locker was empty, but then I saw, right at the back, a small, greyish bundle. I had a premonition we were about to discover something interesting. Ethelred looked ready to pounce, but my hand got there first, as it so often does—it's something you need to *practice*. The small bundle proved to be an old bag made of felt—once, doubtless, a rich blue but now a washed-out blue-grey. Embroidered on it in silver was a double-headed eagle. The bag was pleasingly soft to the touch, but contained something harder. I knew instinctively that I was going to love what I found inside. I took a deep breath, loosened the drawstrings and peered into the aperture.

'Holy shit,' I said. In reply several million Pounds-worth of gemstones winked back at me. I knew that they wanted to be my friends. 'Hello, little diamonds,' I said. 'I'm your new mummy.'

'Holy shit,' said Ethelred over my shoulder. He'd evidently clocked them too. 'I've never even *seen* diamonds that size.'

I smiled modestly. Every mother likes to hear her children praised.

'Elsie,' said Ethelred, 'you know you can't keep those, don't you?'

A vision of myself striding into the London Book Fair in a necklace composed of diamonds the size of plovers' eggs faded. It faded very, very slowly, but it faded all the same.

'Maybe just one? Just the runt of the litter? I reckon I could prise that one out of the setting, and it would never really be missed.' The dazzling reflection from even the smallest of these, I reckoned, could blind any publisher who tried to get the better of me.

'No,' said the spoilsport beside me.

'Let's get these babies back to the hotel anyway,' I said.

'Is that wise?'

'You mean in respect of my taking several million Pounds-worth of stolen diamonds back to a hotel crawling with police who are looking for them?' I asked.

'Yes.'

I thought about it and conceded he might have a point.

'You mean we could get arrested before we have a chance explain that we are the good guys?'

Ethelred considered. 'Yes,' he said. 'Something like that.'

I ran through the logic of this again. There was a flaw in it somewhere, but we were at least agreed on not having the police seize the necklace and arrest us.

'If we leave it here, though,' I said, 'there's a danger Herbie will come back for them. People must lose keys all the time, so it won't be too difficult for him to get somebody to open the locker up for him. We could bury the loot at the crossroads at the dead of night, but we've got a few hours to wait before it will be quite dead enough.'

'Slightly more prosaically,' said Ethelred, 'we could simply switch lockers—to that one over there, say...'

It was the work of a moment to find a new home for my diamonds in 051, leaving an empty 045.

We left the station clutching two keys.

'Stop looking round all the time,' I hissed at Ethelred as we started back towards the hotel.

'There could be somebody following us,' he said.

'Nobody knows we're here,' I said. 'Relax. It's the perfect crime.'

'It's only a crime,' said Ethelred, 'if you're planning to keep the diamonds for yourself.'

'It's clearly Czarist stuff,' I pointed out. 'The Czar's dead. That means it's Finders Keepers.'

'It just happens to be in a bag with a double-headed eagle on it. It could be Austro-Hungarian for all you know. Europe in those days was awash with mutant birds of prey. Anyway, Finders Keepers is not an established legal principle.'

'Don't the poor little diamonds get any say in all this?'

'No.'

Ethelred can be really unreasonable at times.

We approached the garden wall cautiously, but there was no policeman outside. The side street was deserted. We paused briefly as a car passed by on the main road, then I crouched down and replaced Herbie's key in the wall, and stopped up the crack with fresh dirt.

Yes, it had all been a bit too easy.

Still, nobody stopped us as we re-entered the hotel. Nobody questioned us as we went into the bar. Herbie was already there, clutching the smallest beer on earth. I was tempted to phone the Guinness Book of Records. We nodded to him in a friendly way. He oiled across the room to us, his grip still firmly on his drink.

'I get the impression,' he said in a low voice, 'that we are not being watched as closely as we were.'

I couldn't see that I owed Herbie any favours, so I replied noncommittally.

He looked from side to side. 'See anyone out there in the garden?'

'I don't remember,' I said.

'Still, I reckon the old security's not as tight as it was.'

'If you say so,' I said.

'I do say so, Elsie. I might just take a stroll round,' he said with what he could have imagined was devious cunning. 'Get some fresh air.'

'Don't let me stop you,' I said.

After he'd gone, Ethelred looked at me as though I was an idiot. 'Why didn't you say you thought we were still being watched? He'll be digging the key out of the wall and will be off to the station straight away.'

'And I'd like to see his face when he gets there,' I said. 'I'd like to see him opening the locker and finding nothing.'

'It was still silly,' said Ethelred.

'Not when I have the right key safely in my pocket,' I said.

I removed it and placed it on the table.

'There we are,' I said. 'Key number 051.'

We both looked at it with some interest.

'That's key number 045,' said Ethelred.

'Good point,' I said. 'So it is.'

I bought Ethelred a large brandy. It was the least I could do. I then sneaked off back to my room, while Ethelred was still merely speechless with rage. I reckoned that the mellowing influence of twenty-year-old cognac would not have its full effect for a good half hour, after which it might be safe to return and discuss the next step in a rational manner.

As I walked up the stairs, however, I began to mull things over. Obviously by now Herbie was either clutching my poor baby diamonds or had already hidden them rather better than last time. I was resigned to that. But thinking about it, hadn't Ethelred's behaviour been a bit odd? I mean, he was the one who thought that the diamonds should be returned to their proper, legal owners. So, the best way to do this was to hide them in another left luggage locker, a few feet to the left of the first one? No, on reflection, probably not. Obviously, I had thought conceal-ment was a good plan, but shouldn't Ethelred be handing the diamonds over to the police round about now, while they praised him for being the upright citizen that he was? And shouldn't he, now that things had not gone quite according to Plan A, be alerting the police to the fact that a weasel was heading for the station with key 051 in his hand and malign intent? Obviously Herbie could be stopped, but Ethelred wasn't figuring to stop him any time soon. Was Plan B to let Herbie have the diamonds anyway? These, then, were the things I was pondering as I made my way back along the gloomy corridor to my room at the remote end of the hotel.

And I would have gone on pondering for a while, had a hand not emerged unexpectedly from the shadows and dragged me by the neck into a secluded alcove. As my head smashed sickeningly against the flock wallpaper, it briefly occurred to me that things really weren't going my way.

CHAPTER 26

As you probably know, when your head is smashed against the flock wallpaper of a damp and gloomy hotel in the Loire Valley, a number of thoughts go through your mind:

1. Mmm, flock wallpaper—I didn't know they made that any more
2. I wonder who is doing this to me?
3. And why?
4. Ouch
5. Mmm, flock wallpaper—I didn't

I was probably out cold only for a few seconds, but it was long enough to forget why I had decided to lie on the floor. Herbie Proctor's face hovering a few inches above my own was a puzzling phenomenon that I could link only tenuously with the blinding headache that I had somehow acquired.

'Get up!' he hissed, dragging me to my feet.

I was still a bit woozy, so I fell back against a wall, which somebody had thoughtfully placed behind me. Somebody (the same person or another) needed to explain to me what was going on. It was like one of those quizzes where you have to think of as many capital cities as you can beginning with 'T' (say) in thirty seconds and suddenly you realise you can't think of any. What you need is another couple of minutes to get your act together but thirty seconds is all you've got. And my thirty seconds (or whatever the rules were) was suddenly up.

Herbie had one sweaty paw on my arm and the other covering my mouth. I wondered if it was the fleur de lys pattern on the wall-paper that was making me feel sick. I needed to think fast.

'Don't scream,' he said.

Up to that point I had not considered screaming, though I had thought quite seriously about throwing up.

'Wherrrr sherr dherrr shrerr,' I said, not unreasonably.

He took his hand off my mouth.

'Why should I scream?' I asked.

Actually the main reason for screaming was that he was now pinning me against the wall in a way that was getting just a bit too personal.

'Is that a gun in your pocket or are you just pleased to see me?' I asked.

'It's a gun,' he said.

He was looking at me with distaste, but perhaps he just didn't like Mae West quotes. And I was still reasonably sure that the bulge was his mobile phone.

'You think you're pretty clever, don't you?' snapped Herbie.

I tried to remember—I thought the answer was probably 'yes' but I wasn't sure. What game were we playing? If this was a pub quiz, I really needed Ethelred there.

'I don't think I know what you're talking about,' I said. 'My head hurts too much.'

'I'm talking about this,' snarled Herbie. A small key was waved in front of my face. It was sort of familiar. It bore the number 051.

'It's a key,' I said. It wasn't much of a guess, but my head was thumping and I was fairly sure that I had the pattern of the flock wallpaper imprinted on my forehead.

'But it's not *my* key,' said Herbie. 'Did you think you'd get away with it? Did you think I wouldn't check? My key was numbered 045. Somebody replaced the key that I had hidden with this key. So, I wondered...who could have seen me hiding the key? Who would have taken my key and replaced it with this one? Who would that be, Elsie?'

I was still sufficiently dazed that I wanted to know too.

'Me?' I suggested. The clue seemed to be in the question.

'Yes, you,' he said.

I closed my eyes to see if the pain would go away, just a little. It didn't. To make things worse, when I opened my eyes, I was staring at a small revolver. This spoilt the mobile phone theory. I was more worried that the gun might go off accidentally than that Herbie would actually shoot me, but I was a bit worried about the actual shooting thing too.

'The moment I discovered the keys had been switched,' Herbie was saying, 'I knew it was you. So, I came straight back to retrieve what was mine. Now—since this is your key—where exactly have you hidden mine? If you think you're Mae West, it's probably down the front of that blouse.'

The possibility that he might test this hypothesis empirically concentrated my mind wonderfully. Suddenly I was able to focus on matters at hand.

'It's in my *pocket*,' I said.

'Hand it over.'

'And if I refuse?'

He released the safety catch on the revolver. OK, so *now* it could go off accidentally. In one sense, Herbie's threat was as empty as his locker. His gun, even to my untrained eye, lacked a silencer. It would make a loud bang when he fired it. While I was not keen on loud bangs at present, even a single gunshot would prove fatal to his own plans. He wouldn't get to the stairs before a number of resident policemen converged on this corridor, curious to learn who was shooting at whom.

But for these to be valid considerations, your gunman has to be behaving rationally. There was no indication that Herbie was. The thought occurred to me that these could be my last minutes—in just a moment I could be lying in the corridor of a third rate hotel with a hole in my head. I wasn't keen on either the time or place.

The good news was that my brain's reflex action was to beg for mercy. The bad news was that my mouth was too dry to be able to pass on the message to the man with the gun.

Herbie Proctor pressed the barrel against my right temple. It was uncomfortable, but that didn't seem to bother him. I wondered what it would feel like as the bullet entered my brain. Not good, probably. I summoned up my reserve supply of saliva.

'OK,' I said, though not in a voice I recognised. 'You win, Mr Proctor. We'll swap keys.'

I felt in my pocket and handed him key 045. He smiled, and the safety catch clicked again.

'And there is your key,' he said, almost as an afterthought, handing me 051. 'Now, since we both have our own keys again, I will go on my way.'

I pocketed 051. I tried to look really sad. Even with a splitting head, I suspected I must be smirking.

Herbie regarded at me with contempt. 'You must think I'm really stupid,' he said.

'Piss off,' I said, 'and leave me and my headache alone.'

After he had gone I checked the key again. The number on the ring was still 051. Well, that had almost been worth the pain.

I went to find Ethelred.

Ethelred was still sitting, clutching his fine old brandy and reading a fine old copy of the *Times*. He looked at me curiously as I entered the room.

'Why do you have a fleur de lys imprinted on your forehead?' he asked.

'I ran into a wall,' I said.

'OK,' he said. He returned to reading his paper.

'I'd hoped for some evidence of sympathy,' I said.

'Poor wall,' he replied without looking up.

I produced key number 051 and dangled it in front of his eyes.

'What is the number on this key?' I asked.

He leaned back to get a better focus and almost choked.

'How did you get that?' he asked. 'I mean, *how* did you get that?'

'I met up with Herbie Proctor in the corridor,' I said. 'There was a bit of a scuffle, and I came away with this.'

Well, that seemed a truthful summary of what had happened. No point in overburdening Ethelred with detail.

'You didn't hurt him?' Ethelred asked anxiously.

'I'm marked for ever with French heraldry and you are asking after Herbie's health?'

'I don't want you arrested for assault—at least, not until you get my credit cards back for me.'

'He's fine. He's heading for the station with key 045.'

'And when he gets there?'

'He'll open the locker and find it empty.'

'And then?'

'He'll be pretty sorry he let me have key 051. He will realise that he is a total dipstick and that I am the Queen of Amateur Detectives. Eat your heart out Jane-sodding-Marple.'

'And after he has done that?'

'Ah, yes…'

The lockers were strong, no doubt, but Herbie was, as we had now established, a jewel thief. Were the flimsy station lockers stronger than a hotel safe, for example? Much though you'd like the answer to be 'yes', you had to admit it was probably 'no'.

Would he remember that my key bore the number 051? You'd like the answer to be 'no' but...

Well then, it seemed we were basically back to where we were before, but perhaps this time with a few more minutes in hand. And the advantage of having the right key.

'If we ran...' I said.

'We'd better get a move on,' said Ethelred.

We were out in the street again in about thirty seconds, but Herbie had a good five minutes start on us and looked quite athletic in a rabbity sort of way.

'Why,' said Ethelred, 'do you insist in wearing those high heels? They'll slow us down and we'll end up getting arrested.'

'If we get arrested,' I pointed out reasonably, 'I want to look my best.'

Actually, we were making pretty good time, and there was no need for Ethelred to whinge. As we trotted briskly into the station I saw Herbie at the ticket window.

'*J'ai perdu ma clé,*' he was saying. '*Je vous en prie d'ouvrir la boite pour moi—la boite cinquante et un.*'

'*Pas possible,*' came the stock response from an invisible official. '*C'est absolument défendu.*' Like I've always said, I love bureaucracy. I wish there was more of it. I really do.

'Can I be of help?' I asked, tapping Herbie on the shoulder.

'No,' said Herbie.

'*Non,*' said the invisible official.

'It's just,' I said in my sweetest and most reasonable tones, 'that I overheard this gentleman asking you to open locker number 051 for him. "What a coincidence!" I said to myself. My locker is also 051! So how could it be that this gentleman wishes you to open it up?'

'You have the key?' enquired the invisible official.

'But of course,' I said.

'Stay out of this, Elsie,' said Herbie. He was trying to sound threatening for my benefit and perfectly reasonable for the benefit of the nice bureaucrat. It's not something most people can do, and Herbie was no exception.

'The two of you know each other?' asked the ticket person, leaning forward to see us both.

'One of my very oldest and dearest friends,' I said.

'You are both English?'

'Absolutely,' I said.

'Then, *monsieur*,' she said to Herbie, 'I will leave the two of you to sort this out.'

'Thank you,' I said.

'My pleasure,' said the ticket person. 'By the way, I really like that fleur de lys imprinted on your forehead.'

It was at this point that Ethelred thankfully hove into view, a broad grin over his silly face. I hoped Herbie was in fact more stupid than he looked, because Ethelred's face was yelling, 'Hi, gang! I've switched the lockers again!' at the top of its voice.

'I need a word with you two,' said Herbie with an honest and friendly smile. 'Let's go back to the left luggage room, where we won't be overheard.'

Somewhere a voice in my head was telling me not to trust him, but I was way ahead of mere voices.

'I think we'll just go back to the hotel,' I said. 'I don't think I mind being overheard. Having other people around would be good. The more the merrier.'

'Absolutely,' said Ethelred.

Was this the point to say something to Ethelred about the gun?

The voices were telling me to get my arse out of there right now. There was a whole chorus of them now. They were unanimous.

'I think Ethelred may want to stay,' said the weasel, 'when I tell him that I have a message from a mutual friend.'

'Who?' asked Ethelred, suddenly transfixed.

'I think you know,' said Herbie. 'Our Mutual Friend. Come into the locker room and I'll explain.'

'OK,' said Ethelred.

'Ethelred, we need to get back,' I said, giving his linen sleeve a tug.

But he stood there transfixed. He looked like a small and not particularly bright rodent hypnotised by a snake.

'He's got a gun,' I hissed, though Herbie could hear me as well as Ethelred, and already knew he had a gun, so I might as well have yelled it. 'And whatever it is you think he's saying, it's a lie.'

'That's fine,' said Ethelred distantly. He was already edging towards the left luggage lockers. He now resembled a small rodent that is stupid enough to walk, out of the goodness of its dear little heart, straight into the open jaws of an awaiting snake. Except no known rodent is actually that stupid.

The voices were telling me to leave the silly tosser and save my own skin. You currently got a more despicable class of supernatural advice round here than you did in Joan of Arc's time.

'OK, it looks as though we're in this together,' I said. 'Let's go to the locker room and get it over with.'

'That's very wise,' smiled the weasel.

I tried to hear what the voices inside my head were telling me, but all I picked up was a snort of derision.

CHAPTER 27

The room was not large. It contained, I guessed, around a hundred lockers, each made of unpainted white metal. The unlocked ones could be distinguished by the round, red key tags that dangled prominently from them. Enough were locked however to provide Proctor with what was going to be a good guessing game, once he had told me what I needed to know. I doubted that he had a gun in anything other than his imagination, but my plan would cover that unlikely eventuality.

Elsie was looking at me as though I was stupid, but she had only half the story or (hopefully) less.

As soon as we were inside and the door to the room was closed, Proctor turned, the smile suddenly absent from his face. Not a pleasant face at the best of times, this version was distinctly ugly.

'Right, Ethelred,' said Proctor. 'The key to whichever locker has the diamonds in it. Now, please.'

'Message first,' I said.

'Key first,' he said.

'I don't think so,' I said.

'I have a gun,' he said.

'Which you will not be able to use here,' I said.

'Don't depend on it.'

I smiled. Though Elsie was looking at me as if I were an idiot, my guess was that Proctor had no gun with him.

'I'll risk it,' I said.

'Fine,' said Proctor. 'Have it your way. The message is that your friend looks forward to meeting you in London. In the meantime you are to trust me and hand over the necklace.'

'That's it?'

'That's it.'

'And I am to give you the diamonds on the basis of that?' I asked.

'Isn't that the assurance you want? Your friend is very keen to see you again. But only if you let me have the necklace now.'

'And what will you do with it?' I asked.

'It will be delivered to its rightful owners and your friend will be very pleased with you. Very pleased indeed.'

'Would one of you dickheads stop talking in riddles,' demanded Elsie, 'and say something that a normal person could understand? By the way he *does* have a gun, Ethelred.'

'Clearly we both wish to keep my friend happy,' I said to Proctor. 'I'll tell you what: you can pick the key you prefer.'

Proctor looked puzzled, until I produced four keys and arranged them on the palm of my hand.

'Which locker do you think it is?' I asked.

Proctor shook his head. 'I'm not playing games, Ethelred. Listen to Elsie on the subject of guns and just give me all four keys.'

I handed them over. Obviously he didn't have a gun, but it really made little difference.

'Good boy,' said Proctor, clasping the keys. 'God, you must think I'm stupid.'

As he began to examine what was now in his hand, I gave Elsie's arm a tap and nodded in the direction we should move. Proctor looked up briefly only as we were going out through the door. We dodged round the corner and into the station forecourt.

A taxi had just pulled up and a passenger was paying the driver. I bundled Elsie into the cab and said 'Drive!'

The taxi driver, who was unfamiliar with the conventions of detective fiction, simply turned, a cigarette dangling from his lip. 'Where to?'

I reckoned Proctor would be on his second locker by now.

'Just drive,' I said, glancing over my shoulder.

'How can I just drive? You have to drive in a certain direction. I need to know which direction you wish to go in.' He removed the cigarette and flicked ash, partly out of the window, but mainly over himself.

'Apollinaire,' said Elsie, 'as fast as you can.'

'Why didn't you say so?' He jettisoned the cigarette and carefully adjusted his rear-view mirror. On his third attempt he found the right gear and we began to creep forward.

It was as the taxi completed a leisurely swing across the fore-court that we saw Proctor emerge from the station. He looked like a man who had just suffered another of a long line of disappointments. He yelled something after us, but we never did find out what it was. It was probably quite heart-felt.

'I assume there is a fifth key?' said Elsie, settling back in the seat.

I nodded. 'Something like that.'

'So, the diamonds are perfectly safe?'

I nodded.

'In another locker?'

'Proctor is certainly not going to find them any time soon.'

'I suppose,' said Elsie, 'that you now plan to hand the neck-lace over to the police?'

'Eventually.'

She looked me in the eye. 'That was a test, Tressider,' she said slowly, 'and you have just failed it. If you really planned to hand the diamonds over, you would have them in your pocket now to deliver to the authorities. "Eventually" is no sort of answer at all. All this time you've been saying that *I* can't keep the diamonds, I had assumed that your intentions towards them were at least honourable. Now we have established they are not, tell me, what exactly *are* your plans for my diamonds?'

'To return the necklace to its rightful owners,' I said.

'Minus a couple for us?' she said hopefully. 'I'm sure one or two were loose in their setting, or could be made loose with only a small amount of effort.'

'No,' I said.

'Well, we should at least be negotiating a large reward,' she said.

'Virtue is its own reward, Elsie,' I said.

'Money is its own reward,' said Elsie. 'Virtue is merely a bargaining point.'

'I prefer my virtue unsullied,' I said.

Elsie cocked her head to one side and appeared to be listening to something.

'The voices in my head,' she said, 'have just informed me that you are a silly tosser. And everything my voices say is true.'

Fortunately at this point we drew up in front of Apollinaire, and Elsie's mind turned instantly to more pressing matters. In silence and with respectful demeanour, we prepared to enter the holiest chocolate shrine this side of the Belgian frontier.

Elsie took her time making her selections. She had a good eye for how many chocolates would fit into a given *ballotin* without risk of damage. She would add two of a particular type then, reluctantly, discard one to permit the addition of an even more essential variety. Strangely, she included no peach truffle.

When the ribbon had been tied and the chocolates paid for, we left the shop and headed back towards the hotel. Across the road, leaning conspicuously against a wall, was Herbie Proctor. He sneered as we went on our way.

'He obviously had no difficulty in tracking us down,' I said.

'He probably just grabbed the next cab and said "follow that taxi",' said Elsie. There was a note of regret in her voice that she had not been able to do the same.

'More likely,' I said, 'he just worked out that we were bound to end up at Apollinaire.'

'He's still an arsehole,' said Elsie. She clearly still resented that she had not been permitted to utter one of the great clichés of crime fiction. Then slightly more nervously she added: 'Is he following us?'

'Yes,' I said. 'But what can he do?'

'Ethelred, he really does have a gun,' said Elsie.

'He'd be crazy to use it,' I said.

'He *is* crazy.'

We quickened our pace. So did Proctor.

To be honest, tailing us was not that difficult. Since Proctor knew we had seen him, he did not need to remain concealed. The only possible doubt in his mind would have been whether we were returning to the hotel or whether we were going to double back to the railway station. He was pretty certain we were not going to the police. We did not have an awful lot of options at our disposal.

This part of Chaubord was a narrow cluster of buildings between the Chateau and the Loire. The houses were picturesque, white- or grey-walled, green- or blue-shuttered, with plenty of provincial charm but offering little by the way of cover. A chilly mist was settling over the river and shrouding the pollarded willows on the far bank, but it would have to get a lot thicker to be any use to us.

We ducked into a side street, hoping that we could take another turning before Proctor regained sight of us. We found ourselves in a short but picturesque cul de sac. The uneven tarmac sloped down gradually to the cold and fast flowing Loire. There had possibly been a ferry across the river at this point at one time. Now it was just a deserted dead end. The only two houses flanking the road were closely shuttered. Had we wanted to find a good spot to be shot and pushed into some swirling brown water, we could not have done better.

Proctor too had turned the corner and now stood at the top of the slope, grinning. He started to advance towards us.

'I don't fancy swimming, so I hope you've got a good plan,' said Elsie. 'Or at least a better plan than walking into a death trap and waiting to get shot.'

'You can't shoot somebody with a mobile phone,' I said.

'I've *seen* the gun,' said Elsie.

'Why didn't you say so?'

'I did.'

We had some unlikely saviours. A small posse of motor scooters swung off the main road and towards us. They screeched to a halt just short of the water. One of the riders, aged about twelve as far as I could tell, took out a packet of *Gitanes* and ostentatiously lit up. The cul de sac was, it seemed, where the local youths went to go and do whatever they wanted to do without undue interference from the local police. They might have regarded a double shooting as entertainment or they might have resented somebody encroaching on their patch. Herbie took a look at them, sneered and strolled slowly back. We followed cautiously.

The three of us rejoined the main road more or less together.

'Are you going back to the hotel?' I asked Proctor.

He raised an eyebrow but said nothing. Elsie and I set off again along the main road, Proctor following ten yards or so behind. The occasional car passed by, giving us some sort of security, but not much. For the first time ever I was hoping to see some more delinquent teenagers.

The road was flanked mainly by houses, which formed a solid, grey terrace along the narrow pavement. Nothing offered any refuge until we reached a bookshop; we ducked inside.

Proctor strolled past. The message in his glance was simple. We could look at books if we wished. He could get us any time.

'Now do you believe he is the murderer?' demanded Elsie, replacing the copy of Proust, in which she had rather improbably been engrossed, back on the shelf.

'Maybe,' I said.

'Hold on,' said Elsie. 'Which other guest has assaulted me with a wall? Which other guest has threatened us both with a gun or (if you insist) loaded mobile phone? Which other guest, apart from us obviously, has had stolen Czarist stuff in his or her possession? Which other guest has tailed us in a menacing manner? Which other guest has lied so consistently and unconvincingly?'

All of this was true, and I was beginning to question my certainty that I knew who the killer was. The reason that I had doubted Proctor's guilt was that there was no logic to killing Davidov *after* stealing the gems. But why should I be looking for logic? Fictional crime is logical. Real life crime is too often sad and haphazard. As Margaret Williams had commented after stabbing her other half: 'If the knife hadn't been on the table my husband wouldn't be dead.' But it had been, and he was.

Davidov's death did not need to be necessary—merely possible. Proctor had had plenty of opportunity to murder both of them and the diamonds were a perfectly adequate motive. In the same way, Proctor had no need to kill me, but on the other hand...

'I think we should continue on our way,' I said. 'Even if we run into Proctor, there should be plenty of other people around all the way back to the hotel.'

'And then?' asked Elsie.

'We'll be fine,' I said. 'Herbie has shot his bolt.'

'I'm glad you think so,' said Elsie. 'Maybe you would like to tell me why you are so damned sure and what you know about Herbie Proctor that I don't?'

'Herbie Proctor? Nothing at all.'

'You have a mutual friend.'

'I don't think he's a friend of hers exactly,' I said.

Elsie looked at me. 'So, who is this female friend...of yours?'

'Nobody you know,' I said.

'Ethelred, I can tell when you are lying,' said Elsie.

I smiled enigmatically. I doubt that the Sphinx could have done a better job. For the moment she was simply guessing.

'I'll find out sooner or later,' she said.

That, conversely, was probably true. The main thing, however, was that she did not do anything stupid in the meantime.

Getting back into the hotel was no more difficult than before. I nudged open the gate and peered into the garden. Nobody was sitting on the terrace. Nobody was patrolling the grounds. We slipped in and nonchalantly strolled up the steps.

'Why isn't anyone watching us?' I asked.

'We're no longer suspects,' said Elsie.

'That's the simplest answer,' I agreed.

'Is Herbie around?'

'I don't see him,' I said, taking a quick look round, 'but he knows where he can find us.'

'I wish he didn't,' Elsie said.

'He wouldn't try anything here,' I said.

'Ethelred, he *did* try something here,' Elsie said, pointing to her forehead.

'You can hardly see it now,' I reassured her. 'Just a little red spot.'

'Maybe,' said Elsie, 'we should report him to the police anyway.'

'Maybe later,' I said.

'Later? Isn't that a bit like "eventually"? There's a pattern developing here, Tressider. What you're saying is that you don't want any contact with the police.'

'I don't think Herbie Proctor is a threat,' I said. 'Not to us, anyway.'

'That may be what you and your friend reckon,' said Elsie. 'But she's not here. In the meantime, I think you and I should stick closely together, just in case.'

'Look,' I said, 'I need to make a call. You'll be fine here in the bar.'

'Make the call here, Tressider,' she suggested.

I took out my phone and flipped it open and shut it again quickly. 'Sorry—no can do. The signal's lousy,' I said. 'I'll be back in a second.'

I found myself a secluded spot, completely free of literary agents. I took from my pocket a crumpled piece of paper with a number on it in pencil. Then I dialled and waited for a response.

'Hello,' said a voice after a cautious pause.

'It's me, it's Ethelred,' I said.

'Are you back in London?'

'Not yet.'

'Then you are not supposed to phone this number,' said the voice. 'I'm hanging up now. Goodbye.'

'But I do have the diamonds,' I said quickly.

There was a silence. Nobody hung up.

'Who said anything about diamonds?' the voice demanded. 'I've no idea what you are talking about.'

'So you don't want them, then?'

'Describe them,' said the voice dryly.

'Big,' I said. 'Very big. They're in a blue felt bag. It's faded, as you might expect after all these years. It has a double-headed eagle embroidered on it.'

There was a brief silence that was more eloquent than anything she might have said.

'You do actually have them, then?'

'I know where they are, which is something nobody else currently knows.'

'Don't play games with me, Ethelred. I don't have the time.'

'Nobody's playing games. Not here. Do the names Grigory Davidov and Jonathan Gold mean anything to you?'

There was another silence.

'No,' said the voice.

'So, it won't trouble you that both have been murdered?'

'Oh, holy *shit*! You idiot! How did you let that happen? Where? When?'

'At the hotel, a couple of days ago. And I could hardly have mounted a twenty four hour guard on them even if I had known that I had responsibility for ensuring their safety.'

'Do I need to explain everything to you?'

'Explaining even a little would have been helpful,' I said.

'Just get out of there and back to London.' She had quickly regained her composure. The deaths had been noted, considered and dismissed. Her tone had reverted to its normal one of impatience and mild irritation at everything I did or said.

'None of us can leave the hotel because the police are still investigating,' I pointed out. 'Hang on!'

I said these last words because I thought I heard noises off. I listened more carefully, but there was nothing untoward. Just the usual distant but reassuring sounds of hotel activity, and a lorry passing in the street. I was clearly getting jumpy.

'Hang onto what?' my phone was demanding.

'Nothing. It's fine. Where was I?'

'You were saying that a couple of hotel guests had been murdered. Tedious for you, and for them, but of no great concern to me. Purely out of interest, who killed them?'

'I wondered if you could tell me that?'

'Me? Of course I can't. The police don't suspect *you*, do they?'

'Maybe briefly.'

'How briefly?' There was renewed concern in her voice, though possibly not on my account.

'Very briefly indeed.'

'And the diamonds are completely safe?'

'Yes.'

There was a sigh of relief.

'Then all you have to do, Ethelred, is sit it out. Even you should be able to manage that.'

'A guy named Herbie Proctor's trying to get the diamonds from me,' I said. 'He claims to know you.'

'He mentioned my name?'

'I don't think there's any doubt who he meant. What exactly is his role in all this? Did he kill Davidov or Gold?'

'I wouldn't think so. I don't imagine he does murder—or he's never been caught if he does.'

'So, he's a friend of yours?' I said.

'He's not on my Christmas card list.'

'If you have any influence with him, it might be helpful to ask him not to point a gun in my direction.'

'He's waving a gun around in a hotel full of policemen?'

'More or less.'

'I'll have a word with him.'

'Is he the contact I was supposed to meet?'

'You don't need to know that anymore—not if you already have the diamonds. Complete change of plan, in fact. It sounds as if Proctor is surplus to requirements. Just bring the diamonds to me. I can deal with them.'

'I'll need to give Proctor the slip.'

'And nobody else suspects you may have them?'

'Only Elsie.'

'Yes, I'd heard Elsie was there.'

'How?'

'The resourceful Mr Proctor asked my advice as to what he should do. I said to get her out of the way. He thought he might be able to charm her over to his side or alternatively to get her arrested for just long enough. It would seem he did neither. Why is she there in the first place?'

'She came to bail me out. My credit cards got cancelled.'

'Don't give me any details. I really don't want to know. You'll need to give her the slip too, then.'

'Didn't Proctor tell you about the murders?' I asked. It seemed an odd omission—unless he was the murderer.

'He just said there had been a bit of trouble and that he would fill me in on the detail later. Why are all you men so useless?'

'I don't know,' I said. It's a question I've often been asked, but I've never been told the answer. 'So what do you want me to do?'

'Sit it out, like I say. Bring the diamonds to the address you were given. Don't give them to the idiot Proctor. Don't let the idiot Proctor get arrested or God knows what he'll tell people. Don't tell that other idiot Elsie any more than she needs to know. She's a nosy cow, but fortunately not that bright. And don't phone this number again.'

'One other thing...' I began.

The voice was replaced by a low buzzing noise. There was no more to say, in somebody's opinion anyway. Still, at least I knew what I had to do. That always makes things easier, in my experience.

CHAPTER 28

It's one thing dodging into shops to avoid a crazed killer with a loaded mobile phone. It's quite another running into them again at the hotel and trying to make small talk as if nothing much had happened. And if there's one lesson I've learned from horror films it's that *you don't split up*. Especially if you are the cute, cuddly one. In real life you don't always get the spooky music to tell you when the guy with the chainsaw, three days' stubble and a chip on his shoulder is closing in on you, but in all other respects, the rules are identical. And it's always the cute cuddly one that gets it.

With Ethelred by my side, therefore, it all felt quite safe and comfortable. The moment he went off to make a phone call, I got a bit edgy. It felt like that brief moment of silence before the spooky music starts up.

It was for that reason—and, I must stress, for that reason alone—that I sort of drifted after Ethelred. He had ensconced himself in the breakfast room, which was empty at that time of day. I thought that the best thing would be to stand just outside the room, so as not to distract him in any way. I tried hard not to listen to the conversation that he was having, but he was whispering quite loudly. As so often is the case, he had only himself to blame.

'So you don't want them, then?' he was saying as I took up my position.

There was a pause as he listened intently, a bit like a dog glued to the every word of its master. Or mistress.

'Big,' he said. 'Very big. They're in a blue felt bag. It's faded, as you might expect after all these years. It has a double-headed eagle embroidered on it.'

So it was about the diamonds? But who else, other than dead people, me and Herbie, knew about them?

'I know where they are,' Ethelred added, 'which is something nobody else currently knows.'

Well, I knew, surely? They were at the station. He had certainly implied they were at the station. Or was he playing games?

'Nobody's playing games,' he went on. 'Not here. Do the names Grigory Davidov and Jonathan Gold mean anything to you?'

It was at this point that the nice Danish lady hove into view. She looked determined to talk to somebody. It would clearly have been inconvenient to have held a discussion with her there and then, unless it could be conducted in a whisper or by sign language, which I doubted. I therefore slipped further down the corridor before she could spot me, but in the process lost audio contact with Ethelred. A couple of minutes passed before I was sure that she had passed on her way. I tiptoed back again to my post outside the breakfast room door. Ethelred was fortunately still speaking, but I'd clearly missed a bit—possibly a crucial bit.

'Only Elsie,' Ethelred was saying in a resigned sort of way.

Me? Little me? My ears pricked up. They now had every right to do so. I took the risk of peeping round the corner. Ethelred was standing with his back to me, looking out of a window.

'She came to bail me out,' he said as if he had to apologise for my presence rather than express his joy and eternal gratitude. 'My credit cards got cancelled.'

True. But it was his own fault. Possibly somebody was telling him that, because he did not look entirely happy.

'So what now?' he said sulkily.

Ethelred listened carefully, but still did not seem entirely content.

'One other thing...' he started. Then he stopped dead, his mouth open as if to form the final missing words. For a long time he stood there, with the phone still to his ear, not speaking. He seemed very, very thoughtful—a bit like that Master's Voice dog you used to see on records, but without the gramophone. At last he snapped the phone closed, turned on his heel and thus came face to face with me. This did not please him as much as it should have done.

'What are you up to?' he demanded suspiciously.

'Can't a girl take a stroll?' I asked.

'Yes,' he said. 'As long as she does not listen to other people's conversations.'

'Was there anything interesting to listen to?'

'No.'

'Then it wouldn't have mattered if I was listening, would it?'

'How long had you been there, Elsie?'

'Just arrived,' I said brightly.

'Why didn't you stay put in the bar?'

'I got nervous. Plus, I've probably got post-traumatic stress syndrome or something. Plus I needed the loo. Plus...' I paused. One good, partially-true reason is often more convincing than a stream of consciousness collection of lies. Under normal circumstances I might have simply flounced off at this point, leaving Ethelred to guiltily work out how he had offended me, but then I remembered Herbie Proctor. And the gun.

'Anyway, I've found you now,' I said taking Ethelred's arm. 'Shall we return to the bar?

I stayed pretty close to Ethelred for the rest of the afternoon. I was obliged to concede that Ethelred was occasionally allowed

to desert me to visit the lavatory or perform some other necessary task. It was during one of these short absences that Taylor
deposited himself in a nearby chair.

'What I miss most,' he said in a confidential manner, 'is
chocolate. The moment they let us out I'm off to Apollinaire.'

He hadn't struck me as a chocolate-head and he went up a
notch or two in my estimation.

'You, me and Mr Davidov,' I said. 'We could have had our
own chocolate conference right here in the hotel.'

'And Jonathan Gold,' he said.

'Gold?'

'Yes, absolutely. I saw him in Apollinaire the day before he
died.'

'Quite slim, Jonathan Gold,' I said.

'Yes,' said Taylor.

'You wouldn't think he ate chocolates at all,' I said.

'No,' said Taylor.

'Of course, some people can eat all the chocolate they want
and get away with it,' I said, thoughtfully.

'Who can?' asked Taylor.

Taylor dropped back several notches in my estimation.

'Some of us,' I said.

'Oh right, you mean yourself,' he said, but too late to qualify
for even one Brownie point.

'Interesting, though, in terms of how Davidov died,' I said.

'Interesting?'

'The chocolate,' I said.

Then I remembered that it was probably not common knowledge that Davidov had been poisoned with chocolate.

'The chocolate is connected in some way to the murders?'
he asked.

'I didn't say that,' I said.

Taylor looked at me oddly, though I was, frankly, getting
used to odd looks.

'I see. Thank you,' he said.

'No, thank *you*,' I said.

'No, thank *you*,' he said.

'Whatever,' I said.

Taylor moved on to do the things he did when he wasn't playing detectives. Still, it all opened up a new line of enquiry. Gold could not have poisoned Davidov (Gold being dead) but he could have passed the chocolates—and maybe the cyanide—to an accomplice, who had proceeded with a pre-arranged plan to poison Davidov. And that person was still in the hotel.

I wanted to talk it all through with Ethelred, but was beginning to wonder if Ethelred wasn't the person concerned. Who were the people that he was going to deliver the diamonds to? And what was Gold's connection with them?

Back to the Internet, then.

This time, sitting in the relative safety of reception, I typed in 'Gold Goldstein diamonds'. As usual the interesting stuff was on page one. Strangely none of it referred to Jonathan Gold, but it did make things clearer. Much clearer.

CHAPTER 29

I was so struck by what I had discovered that I literally bumped into Herbie Proctor as I was returning to the bar. There was nobody else to be seen, but this stretch of corridor was well frequented and the chances of him picking me up and smashing my head into the wall seemed no worse than fifty/fifty. I therefore decided to tough it out.

'Squeak,' I said. Or something very much like it.

He smiled like some sleazy uncle who has had a bit too much Christmas sherry. He was about to ask me to trust him. That would at least give me time to knee him somewhere soft and run.

'Can we go and discuss things quietly?' he suggested.

'Oh, yeah, right,' I said. 'Been there, done that, got the fleur de lys head decoration.'

'But we do need to talk,' he said.

'Whenever I talk to you,' I said, 'I end up arrested or with a splitting headache or both. And that wasn't a mobile phone you pointed at me. Why don't I just scream now and get it over with? Then, why don't I get the police to arrest you for assault?'

'Because you and your friend Ethelred are currently in possession of a bag of stolen diamonds, which you might find it difficult to explain away,' he pointed out.

'The diamonds are not in the hotel,' I said. Ha!

'I rather think they are,' he said. 'Ethelred would not have been so careless as to leave them behind at the station, would he?'

This could be true. Thinking about it, maybe Ethelred had been a little vague about exactly where the diamonds were.

'Ethelred is going to return the diamonds to their rightful owner,' I said, looking Herbie straight in the eye.

'No,' said Herbie, 'I am going to return the diamonds to their rightful owner. Ethelred is planning to arse around with them like a total tit, and then will either get arrested or will mislay the bag on the way back to London.'

Though I still distrusted Herbie, I was obliged to concede, on the basis of past experience, that this probably *was* Ethelred's plan.

'So, what's the deal?' I asked, playing for time.

'We split the profit two ways,' he said.

'I get half the diamonds?'

'No, you get half the *profit*. As I said, I am planning to return the diamonds to their rightful owner, bypassing a certain friend of Ethelred's, who seems to believe she is entitled to a large cut even though she has taken none of the risk. I don't need her now, and the owners will pay me generously enough. I shall give you half of what they give me. After deducting my expenses. Including all meals.'

'Two thirds,' I said.

'No, half,' he said.

'Sixty percent,' I said.

'Half,' he said.

'Fifty five.'

'Half.'

'I admire your negotiating technique,' I said. 'Have you ever worked for a publisher by any chance?'

'No.'

'Fifty two and a half. That's my final offer.'

'Fifty. Exactly half.'

Well, it was more convincing than conceding sixty six percent straight off. Or was that what he wanted me to think?

'Just who are the rightful owners anyway?' I demanded. 'Not Mr Andersen again? Maybe the Brothers Grimm this time?'

'Yes, sorry about that. At that stage we were not working in the same side. Now we are. Nevertheless, you don't need to know who my clients are.'

'But, I'd like to know. Don't you trust me?'

'No.'

'Tell me anyway,' I said with an open and winning smile. 'Fifty percent, but I need to understand who and what I'm dealing with.'

For a few moments we looked each other in the eye. He blinked first.

'It's the Borodin family,' he said. 'That's the truth.'

I looked him in the eye again, just to double-check. There was a small but measurable chance he was not lying.

'Not Goldstein?' I said.

'Not Goldstein. Borodin. They're the legal owners. It's a long story. I'll tell it to you some time—but not now.'

'And exactly what are you expecting me to do?' I asked.

'Ethelred trusts you. Just get him to tell you where the diamonds are now. I'll do the rest.'

'That sounds like the sort of deal that Delilah cut with the Philistines,' I said. 'She came to a bad end—or was that Jezebel? Either way, I'll want more than fifty percent.'

'OK. Fifty one percent,' he said wearily.

'Done,' I said.

I made a mental note to ask Ethelred whether it was Delilah or Jezebel who got eaten by dogs. Hopefully Jezebel.

Proctor looked at me as though that had all been a bit too easy, then said: 'Let me know as soon as you find anything out. In the meantime, maybe we should not be seen together too much.'

'I can live with that if you can,' I said.

Of course, he was not going to get the information because:

1. Giving him the information would have been a betrayal of the agent-author relationship, which is a sacred trust.

2. Nobody who is negotiating seriously agrees to fifty one percent of a total that has yet to be specified.

3. Ethelred did not trust me enough to tell me where the diamonds were.

Still, he was right about one thing. Ethelred probably would do something stupid with the diamonds unless he was watched carefully.

Ethelred was in his bath when I tracked him down again, but he was very pleased to see me nevertheless.

'Oh, for God's sake! This really is the limit, Elsie,' he sighed as he opened the door. 'Whatever you have disturbed me for, it had better be good.'

'You're dripping water all over the carpet,' I said, as I edged past him into his bedroom.

'That's because some moron kept knocking on the door and made me get out of my bath,' he said.

'Those towels are very big, are they?' I said.

He quickly adjusted his towel.

'Can't this wait?' he said, as I made myself comfortable on his bed. 'Stop bouncing up and down like that and tell me what you are here for.'

'Not as springy as my bed,' I said. 'Anyway, I thought you might like to know that Herbie has just propositioned me. He wants me to come over to the Dark Side. What do you think I should do?'

'Whatever you wish,' said Ethelred, heading back towards his bath. 'Just so long as you can do it without my assistance.' I heard various splashings and sighings as he re-immersed himself.

'OK. Thanks. That's very understanding of you, but I do need to ask you one question. Herbie wants me to find out from you where you've hidden the diamonds. He doesn't believe they are at the station, and (thinking about it) nor do I. Once I have found out the true location, he'll do the rest, whatever that is. It probably involves hitting you over the head with a blunt instrument and running away rapidly with a bag of diamonds. So, do you want to tell me where they are? I've got a piece of paper and a pencil here. Fire away.'

The splashings and sighings ceased.

'Did he really say that?' asked Ethelred.

'Yes.'

'And what did you say?'

'I said I wouldn't do it for less than fifty one percent.'

'And you are planning to tell him?'

'Ethelred, you tart, I would hardly be relating all this to you if I planned to team up with the man who has battered me over the head and got me arrested three times. I just thought you might like to know, that's all. Are the diamonds somewhere safe?'

'Yes,' said a voice from the bathroom.

'Have you stupidly tried to hide them in this hotel?'

There was a long pause.

'No,' said a voice from the bathroom.

'Fine,' I continued. 'Now I also need to tell you what I have just discovered on the "Internet".'

'Stop doing that quotation marks thing with your fingers,' said a voice from the bathroom.

'Do you want to know or not?'

'Yes.'

'Yes, what?'

'Please,' said Ethelred.

'Good boy. Now, I needed to find out what the link might be between Gold and the Goldstein diamonds. So I decided, as I say, to conduct a little research on the Internet. It had already thrown up a video of Gold in a crowd of protestors. Gold was asking Davidov about the Goldstein Diamonds. A little more research revealed their history. It goes like this.

'Erasmus Goldstein was a banker in Germany just before the last war and the last known legal owner of the diamonds. He left Germany after Hitler came to power, but wasn't able to get the diamonds out with him. The necklace was known to be in Berlin in the 1940s, but in the chaos at the end of the war it just vanished.

'In one sense, the Goldsteins were not the unluckiest of the necklace's owners. They were safe in London. After the war they tried to trace the diamonds. The Russians were by that time in control of East Germany, but they denied any knowledge. It wasn't a high priority for the British or American military authorities in Berlin either.

'The family followed up any lead they could over the next few years. In the meantime, feeling that Goldstein had a foreign ring to it, they anglicised their name, by the simple expedient of dropping the 'stein' bit at the end. They became the Golds. Jonathan Gold was Erasmus Goldstein's grandson.

'A year or two back, as you told me, the Golds got their best lead for a long time. Davidov's wife was photographed wearing something that was identical to the missing necklace—much to the embarrassment of Davidov, who probably thought that nobody was still looking for it after all this time. Since what we found in left luggage pretty much matches the description on the web, then we almost certainly have in our possession whatever Davidov's wife was wearing. Jonathan Gold seems to have known that the diamonds still existed and where they were. I don't know precisely how they arranged to meet or what the deal was to be, but my guess is that Davidov brought the necklace with him and placed it in the hotel safe in a white envelope.'

There had, during this account, been sounds of a tall crime writer emerging awkwardly from the bath. He issued from the bathroom in a fairly damp hotel dressing gown, towelling his hair in a thoughtful manner.

'So, you're saying that Gold came to the hotel to persuade Davidov to do the decent thing and return the necklace?' he said.

'Or to blackmail him. He was in a position to cause Davidov a great deal of embarrassment,' I pointed out.

'Do oligarchs get embarrassed that easily? Everyone knows he was a fairly shady character. An allegation that he was handling stolen property could have been shrugged off somehow.'

'The football deal was pretty important to him. And he's had people killed for less. Allegedly.'

'I agree that could give Davidov a motive for killing Gold,' he said. 'But I can't see why he'd do the killing himself…'

'I don't think it was as simple as blackmail anyway. If Gold was just after money, Davidov had no need to bring the diamonds with him. He didn't need to prove he had them in order to be blackmailed. But if Davidov *was* planning to hand them over secretly to their rightful owners…' I said.

'So, it's back to Davidov doing the decent thing and returning the family property…'

'…which was an embarrassment to Davidov anyway. He could scarcely sell the necklace on the open market. So, Davidov

meets up with Gold in London to discuss some sort of deal—
hence the receipt.'

'A meal for one?' said Ethelred.

'They both pay for their own. Why not? Then Davidov
arranges to meet Gold here for the handover.'

'But,' said Ethelred, 'one or other of them had second
thoughts about something; they fell out.'

'You seem very sure about that,' I said.

'Just a guess.'

'Ethelred, is there anything you know but haven't told me
about Gold and Davidov?'

'No.'

'OK, then. Maybe they were haggling over the terms of the
handover? If so, it may have caused a fatal delay.'

'Fatal?' asked Ethelred.

'Somebody else was after the diamonds. Somebody who
was willing to kill them both. While they delayed, a third party
stabbed Gold, poisoned Davidov and made off with the stones.'

'But Proctor made off with the stones,' pointed out Ethelred.

'Precisely,' I said.

Ethelred frowned. 'He's a private eye.'

'And Crippen was a doctor. Who says private eyes can't be
murderers?'

'But all the same...'

'In any case,' I said, 'He told me he was working for a family
called Borodin, who were the rightful owners.'

'And?'

'As I said, the rightful owners were the Goldsteins, now
known as the Golds. So he is basically lying, Ethelred. He makes
these names up as he goes along. Almost nothing he has said to
me over the past three days is the truth.'

'Possibly.'

'He had put together a folder of press cuttings about
Davidov.'

'But he may not be the murderer.'

'Ethelred, is there anything that you know but haven't told me about Herbie Proctor?'

'No.'

'OK then. Why shouldn't we shop him?'

'He knows that we have the diamonds. He'll tell the police.'

'Are you saying we should let a murderer loose on society purely for our own financial gain? Under normal circumstances, I'd go along with that, but...'

'What I plan to do with the diamonds has nothing to do with cash.'

'Anyway Proctor's already killed two people to get his hands on these rocks. Don't you think he might just kill us too? And why should the police believe him unless they can actually locate the diamonds. You say that they are safely hidden?'

'Yes.'

'So, even if we tell the police most of the story, you are in the clear, because they won't be able to find them?'

'Possibly—but it would still not be a good plan.'

'Ethelred, is there anything that you know but haven't told me about the diamonds? Last chance.'

'No.'

'OK then. I think my course of action is clear.'

'Elsie, you're not planning to accuse Proctor of murder, are you?'

'No,' I said.

'That's a relief, anyway,' said Ethelred.

Obviously, I *was* planning to accuse Proctor of murder, but, with the diamonds safely concealed, my plan was watertight. Nothing could possibly go wrong.

Unless Ethelred was holding anything back, of course.

I found the Inspector in his little office behind reception. The room was quite tidy. The dirty plates had gone. The improvised ashtrays had been emptied. He was putting papers into folders and generally clearing away. There was an air of something ending.

'I have some interesting information for you,' I said.

He looked up briefly.

'We have gathered all of the information that we need,' he said.

'And you are about to make an arrest?'

'Alas, that will be impossible,' he replied. He smiled apologetically.

'But...'

'The case is closed,' he said.

'Without an arrest?'

'Sometimes there is no arrest,' he said. 'This is one such case.'

Well, I thought, it's a good job the French taxpayer didn't know how little he was getting for his money. It was scarcely two days into the case and they were wimping out. Maigret must have been turning in his grave.

'I have information that will change your mind,' I said. 'Gather everyone together in the dining room.'

'With what aim?' he asked.

'I shall announce who the murderer was.'

'How interesting. You see yourself as Hercule Poirot, no doubt?'

I ignored the irony.

'I saw myself as a rather younger and sexier Jane Marple,' I said.

'You know who the murderers were?' he asked.

'Precisely,' I said.

'Would you not prefer just to explain to me what your suspicions are? In case you are wrong?'

'No, I'd like to do this in public.'

'I would not wish you to make a fool of yourself,' he said.

'Nor would I,' I said.

'Very well, I was planning to get the guests together and to thank them for their patience during the enquiry. It has, I am sure, been very tedious for you all. Under the circumstances, I can allow you five minutes for your own announcement. No more than that.'

And so it was that word went out that all of the hotel guests were to assemble in the dining room in half an hour's time.

They were all going to be pretty impressed.

CHAPTER 30

So, there we were, all gathered in the dining room: two rather sceptical French policemen, looking bored and checking their watches, two tweedy stamp collectors, one complete Danish family, one smirking Herbie Proctor, one blond pharmaceuticals sales rep, one tall but obscure writer of detective stories and, right in the centre, my good self.

The Inspector nodded at me, as if to say, if I was going to do anything, could I do it now please? I cleared my throat. This was going to be my finest hour. They just didn't know it yet.

'As you are aware,' I said, 'I have asked that you should all assemble here in the dining room so that I can reveal to you who murdered Jonathan Gold and Grigory Davidov.'

Some of the guests, who had rather expected the police to lead on this, looked a little surprised. One of the Danish children broke into brief solitary applause. The mother smiled support-ively. Herbie Proctor sniggered in a nasty way. Well, we'd see who was laughing in a moment or two.

'First, however, I shall rule a number of you out,' I said.

Several people nodded at this point. All of the best amateur detectives proceeded in precisely this way. Ethelred was looking distinctly worried, however. I had not warned him of my plans in advance—I thought it would be a nice surprise for him or rather, to put it another way, I didn't want him pissing about, messing things up. But he was looking strangely green. He patted his jacket pocket a couple of times and looked round the room as if he was checking on escape routes.

'For a while,' I said, getting nicely into my stride, 'I did suspect Tim Brown. He claimed to have arrived here by chance. I soon discovered however that his stop had been planned several weeks ago. He was unable to account satisfactorily for his movements that night. He was in the drugs trade and so might have had access to cyanide. This should have made him the prime suspect but there was no motive and no obvious link to either victim. Then I discovered the true reason for his stopover. He had arranged to see his lover, Ian.'

There was a sort of human explosion off to my right and I saw that Tim Brown was on his feet. 'My *lover* Ian?'

'Precisely,' I said.

'What on earth makes you think he was my lover?'

'I overheard you on the phone. You said that it was time you came out. I'm sorry for your wife, of course, but I'm pleased for you and Ian.'

'Were you listening to a private phone call?'

'Yes,' I said.

'Well, serves you right.'

I seemed to have got something slightly wrong, and Tim was suddenly the focus of some mild curiosity, but it looked as if he was about to set the record straight.

'Let *me* explain to *you* what happened,' he spluttered. 'There's no real secret now. As I said, it would all come out soon anyway. I am the marketing manager of (he named a well-known drug company). I'm good at my job. I'd like to think I'm the best. In my position you get contacted by lots of head-hunters who want to make some money recruiting you for one of your rivals. Recently something came up—a really good opportunity for me. You don't necessarily want it to be known you've been talking to a rival firm until it's certain you wish to make the move. As it happened, both the head-hunter and I were over in France at the same time, so we agreed we would meet some place where there was no chance of being spotted by any of my colleagues. So I arranged to see him here on my way back. His name's Ian—OK? We had dinner and he explained the deal. I liked what I heard but had some questions that he needed to refer back to his client. So I hung around until the client's office opened and we had a conference call.'

'The client's office opened in the early hours of the morning?' I snorted. 'Per-lease—we're not going to swallow that.'

'The client is Indian,' said Tim Brown, 'based in Bangalore.'

OK—maybe we were going to swallow that one. I glanced at Ethelred as Bangalore was mentioned, but he just shrugged. His mind was elsewhere. His face had changed from green to grey, but I wasn't sure that was an improvement.

'It would have all been fine if I had not been held up here,' said Brown. 'I would have been back pretty much as planned. Now I'm going to have some explaining to do, but only to my CEO. My wife is absolutely OK with it—looking forward to living in India in fact.'

'Exactly,' I said quickly. 'You had a perfectly good alibi, so I was able to rule you out.'

'As the police did long ago,' said Tim Brown. 'They phoned Ian.'

'That is true,' said the Inspector. 'We phoned Ian. He was very helpful.' He glanced at his watch again and raised his eyebrows.

'Turning,' I said even more quickly, 'to the Pedersens...' (Mrs Pedersen beamed at me) '... it was possible that that events here were linked to the loss of the valuable "ten kroner puce" stamps. The Pedersens had arrived at the hotel while the stamp fair was on and they came from the small town of Nykøbing, where the stamps were sold.'

'No,' said Mrs Pedersen.

'I thought you came from Nykøbing?'

'We do.'

'And the stamps were sold in Nykøbing?'

'Yes, they were.'

'So you come from the town where the stamps were sold?'

'No.'

Ethelred coughed. 'As I've tried to tell you before,' he said, 'there are two Nykøbings—Nykøbing Falster and Nykøbing Mors. The stamps were sold in Nykøbing Falster.' Being able to correct me in this way should have made him pretty pleased with himself, but he still looked sick.

'That's right, and we come from Nykøbing Mors,' said Mrs Pedersen proudly. 'They make the cast-iron wood-burning stoves there. They export them all over the world. My great aunt worked for the company for thirty years. We are famous for our stoves, but not for our stamps. We didn't hear about the stamps until we got here. Falster is a long way, by Danish standards, from Mors, where we live.'

'Oh, right,' I said.

'An easy mistake to make,' said Mrs Pedersen. 'I remember that one of my aunts was buying a train ticket and...'

'Just so,' I said quickly. 'I was aware, however, that you had no motive for murdering Mr Davidov.'

'On the contrary,' said Mr Pedersen. 'You might say I have a very good motive—at least in an official capacity. Grigory Davidov has been responsible for at least one killing in Denmark, though we lack what you might describe as hard evidence. And his activities more generally were a matter of great concern to us. But assassinating oligarchs would have been incompatible with my diplomatic status. My ambassador would not have been pleased.' He gave a little chuckle, in which others joined.

I looked him in the eye. I knew something (courtesy of his daughter) that he might not want revealed. Well, into every life a little rain must fall.

'And what,' I said, 'if I told people that you worked for the Fors-something Efter-whatsit?'

'The *Forsvarets Efterretningstjeneste*?'

'Probably,' I said. 'What if I said that, eh?'

'I don't think you can,' he said. 'But if you *were* able to say it, you would be quite wrong. I work in the Commercial Section of the Danish Embassy. My Ambassador would be happy, I am sure, to confirm that.' He looked as unruffled as it is possible to look. He just had to be a spy.

'We did not suspect him at any stage,' said the Inspector.

'So you are not a Danish secret agent pretending to be a diplomat?' I asked.

I thought, just for a moment, that I caught Pedersen winking at the Inspector.

'No,' said the Inspector. 'We have checked with our own security people. It is as Mr Pedersen says. He works in the Commercial Section of the Embassy.'

'Right,' I said.

'Please do continue,' said the Inspector.

'So, let me turn next to Mr Taylor,' I said. I was aware I was not doing too well so far, but the key to a good detective story is the ending. I fixed Taylor with my gaze. The others were looking at him curiously. I had their attention again.

'Initially,' I said, 'I had no reason to suspect Mr Taylor, though he is a chemist and might have had access to poisons.'

'Hardly—not where I work,' said Taylor with a forced laugh. 'There's little use for cyanide in the soft drinks industry.'

'My suspicions were aroused,' I continued, in spite of some sniggering amongst my suspects, 'when I discovered he was conducting some rather ineffectual amateur detective work.'

'Not that ineffectual,' he said. 'It was me that told you about Gold buying chocolate—remember?'

'Indeed,' I said. But that surely was irrelevant?

The Danish boy whispered to his mother, who said approvingly, '*Ja, Herr Taylor er meget klog, ikke?*'

Something told me that this was not quite the triumph I had planned. My audience, rather than hanging on my every word, was starting to lose confidence in me, though they seemed to think Taylor was pretty good. The Danish boy said something else but this time was shushed by his mother, who glanced quickly in my direction and smiled apologetically.

'So, to cut a long story short, you also ruled me out?' asked Taylor. 'Is that what you want to say?'

I was beginning to lose my thread, but I had indeed ruled Taylor out.

'That's right,' I said rather flatly.

'What a relief,' he said. 'You had me worried there. Just for a moment I thought I might have done it.'

I pressed on. 'I had no reason to suspect Mr Jones,' I said with a friendly nod in his direction.

'Even though he had worked for one of Davidov's companies, which had then defaulted on his pension, leaving him penniless?' asked Ethelred.

'That's a good point,' I said. 'But Mr Jones was unaware of the connection.'

'Are you kidding?' asked Jones indignantly. 'I was certainly well aware of who owned the company.'

'Were you?'

'Yes,' said Jones. 'I didn't kill Davidov though, for all that.'

'Didn't you?'

'No.'

'Are you sure?' I asked.

It seemed a little late to re-open this line of enquiry but, thinking about it, it was a powerful motive.

'Even though you knew that Mr Davidov owned the company?' I said.

'Yes,' said Jones.

'But we do not suspect Mr Jones,' said the Inspector.

'Thank you,' said Jones.

'Right,' I said.

I was aware the room had gone very quiet.

'What about Tressider?' asked Herbie Proctor. 'He just pitches up here, out of nowhere, in the middle of winter. As a crime writer he would know all about poisons. If anyone should arouse suspicions it's him.'

He was right of course. Ethelred's conduct in relation to the diamonds remained a mystery. And he was a dipstick capable of almost any folly if led astray by some floozy with a husky voice and black silk underwear. Still, I wasn't letting Proctor get away with accusing him of murder.

'My client had no links with Davidov or Gold,' I said. 'There isn't shred of evidence to link him to either murder.' I looked at the Inspector, who nodded in a resigned sort of way.

'You do not need to conduct a formal defence, *Mademoiselle* Thirkettle. We accept that *Monsieur* Tressider has no case to answer.'

'So, who did kill Jonathan Gold?' I asked rhetorically.

'Do you really want me to tell you?' said Herbie Proctor, who obviously did not get the concept of rhetorical. 'Why don't we just cut to the chase and...'

'Not so fast,' I said. 'Let's take this a step at a time. We were aware, because we had seen them in conversation, that Davidov and Gold knew each other. What I did not appreciate was how well.'

I paused and surveyed the room. One or two of the guests now at least showed a mild curiosity.

'I decided to conduct a little research on the Internet. What it showed up was that Davidov had some diamonds that had been stolen from Jonathan Gold's family—diamonds now worth many millions of Euros.'

I paused so that people could gasp in amazement, but the Inspector just said: 'Yes, we know all that.'

'What you may not have known though,' I continued, 'was that Davidov and Gold had met up in London to discuss returning the gems. In Davidov's dressing gown pocket, I found a receipt from a kosher restaurant in north London. He had eaten Methuen Trimmings with Noodles.'

'Mehren Tzimmes with Knaidel,' said Ethelred.

'Whatever,' I said. 'Though they professed to dislike each other, and even to dislike me, it was simply a cover. Gold was negotiating the return of the family jewels. Davidov was relieving himself of a potentially embarrassing piece of loot. Before they could complete the transaction, however, both were murdered and the diamonds stolen.'

I paused and looked round the room. Herbie Proctor had his head on one side, trying to work out what I would say next. The Inspector was cleaning his ear out with a ballpoint pen. Only Ethelred was looking at me in horror. He mouthed something at me, then, when I failed to mouth anything back, looked down at the floor, his head in his hands.

'The diamonds,' I continued, 'were in the safe in a white envelope. The killer, having already eliminated Gold and having put a poisoned chocolate in Davidov's box, then took advantage of the receptionist's brief absence to sneak in and pick the lock on the safe. Later he spirited the diamonds out of the hotel. There is your man, Inspector—arrest Mr Proctor!' I stood dramatically pointing my finger Proctor-wards, but nothing happened.

I looked at Proctor, expecting, at the very least, to see beads of sweat on his evil brow, or a pathetic denial taking shape on his nasty lips, but he just looked a bit bored and pissed off. Ethelred, on the other hand looked as though he was fixing to throw up out of sheer terror.

'Do you have any comments, Mr Proctor?' asked the Inspector.

'Elsie,' said Proctor, 'has a very vivid imagination. If I was going to steal some diamonds, I would just steal the diamonds. As you say, it's not a difficult trick picking a hotel safe...so they tell me, anyway. If I'd already got the diamonds, I'd hardly hang around bumping people off after the event. Conversely, I can't see the point in murdering people in advance of the theft, murders tending (as they do) to attract the attention of the police. I've never heard so much rubbish in my entire life.'

'So who did kill Gold and Davidov then?' I demanded. (Not a rhetorical question this time.)

'Let me explain,' said Taylor. 'I've also done a bit of research on this. As you say, the Goldstein diamonds found their way back to Russia in 1945. The Golds knew that much but it was only after the fall of communism that rumours of the necklace's precise whereabouts started to reach the West, and it was only recently that it became clear that Davidov now owned it. They needed somebody to negotiate with Davidov and decided it should be Jonathan Gold.'

'But, hang on,' I said. 'The Golds have a valid claim. They know who's got it. Why not just go through the courts?'

'A very good question,' said Herbie Proctor. 'A very good question indeed.'

'Who's telling this story?' asked Taylor.

'Me,' said Herbie Proctor. 'I do actually know a few things that I haven't gathered from the Internet.'

Taylor shrugged. Proctor took up the story.

'The Gold family, as my amateur detective friend surmises, chose Jonathan Gold to go in and negotiate with Davidov. That was because he had one thing that none of the rest of them had. Up to that point, Jonathan Gold had shown little interest in the diamonds. His cause was the environment. For him, Davidov's crime was Yacoubabad—not ownership of some Czarist necklace. But his work in India had provided him with proof of Davidov's responsibility for the disaster. This would have been more than an embarrassment for Davidov. There was a real threat of arrest and extradition. So, the family's cunning plan was that he should use this information to blackmail Davidov into giving them the diamonds.'

'I can't see that would work,' I said. 'If Jonathan Gold knew, then others who were investigating Yacoubabad would have known too.'

'Either the family didn't think that bit through or Gold was able to reassure them in some way—in any case, it would not have been put to the test. Jonathan Gold had his own plan, which was the mirror image of his family's plan. He was to use the negotiations for the diamonds as a way of getting a chance to put pressure on Davidov about Yacoubabad. And Davidov was keen to meet up.'

'I don't understand,' I said.

'Davidov wanted to get rid of the necklace,' Proctor continued. 'It had little to do with the embarrassment of owning it and a great deal to do with the fact that he was a very superstitious man. He thought it had brought him bad luck and that the solution was to return it to the real owners. But he was also a greedy man. He hoped that the Golds would buy the necklace at a price to be agreed. He was therefore keen to do a deal.'

'How do you know all that?' I asked.

'Trust me, I have every reason to know,' said Proctor. He was about to go on, but then checked himself briefly before adding: 'It doesn't mean that Davidov actually brought the diamonds here, though. Almost certainly not. It would make sense to leave them safely locked away in Russia or somewhere until the deal was done. Stands to reason.'

'On the contrary,' said Jones, 'All of the evidence points to Davidov having shown up here with the diamonds and without any of his usual bodyguards. But, when he and Gold finally got together, things did not go according to plan.'

'Hang on,' I said, 'It wasn't their first meeting. Davidov and Gold had previously met up in London...'

'No,' said Ethelred. 'I've thought that one through. The receipt was a valuable clue, but that's not what it proved.'

'Oh,' I said.

'If relations between them were ever good,' said Taylor, 'they had deteriorated by the evening of Gold's murder. I don't know what Gold's Plan A was—possibly to get Davidov to pay compensation to the survivors of the disaster. Plan B was clearly to poison Davidov, just as Davidov had poisoned the town. I don't know at what point Plan B became the preferred option but Davidov must have realised that this was no longer about a price for the diamonds. Gold represented a genuine danger—at the very least a danger that the truth was going to come out about Yacoubabad; at the worst that Gold might try to kill him. Davidov therefore took a large knife from the kitchen. I've no idea whether he too was planning murder at that stage or whether he was just going to use it to protect himself.'

'What we do know,' interjected Herbie Proctor, 'is that Davidov had spent so much time in the bloody kitchen congratulating the bloody staff on their bloody cooking that his presence there was not something to be remarked upon.'

'So,' Taylor continued, 'Davidov, in his dressing gown, takes a late night stroll along the corridor to Gold's room, the knife rather poorly concealed, for what must have been a pre-arranged meeting. Who knows what was on the agenda? Gold's last attempt to get Davidov to help the people of Yacoubabad? Davidov's last attempt to cut a deal on the necklace? But Gold was never that interested in the diamonds and Davidov was never going to accept responsibility for anything. In the end Davidov stabbed Gold. No logic. No cunning plan. The knife just happened to be there and Davidov was angry or frightened enough to do it.'

'Leaving Davidov covered in blood himself,' I said, pointing to an obvious flaw in this theory. 'The one thing that nobody has suggested is that any blood was found on Davidov. His dressing gown, that you claim he was wearing, was spotless. He hardly had time to send it to the dry cleaners.'

'Davidov sees Gold's dressing gown hanging up,' said Ethelred. 'He takes off his own dressing gown and drapes it over the body. He puts on Gold's dressing gown, in the pocket of which are two Pound coins and a receipt from a restaurant that Gold has visited recently. Then he sneaks back to his room, waking you briefly as he visits the bathroom to wash off any other traces of blood. Later he disposes of the knife in the rubbish that the dustmen collect early the following morning.' This was the longest statement that Ethelred had made since we arrived in the room. But he still didn't look exactly well.

'So Gold is dead,' said the Inspector. 'Who then, I wonder, steals Davidov's envelope with the diamonds in it?' He looked round the room enquiringly.

'That he had the diamonds in that envelope is just Mr Jones' theory,' said Herbie Proctor. 'I don't share it myself.'

'Quite,' said Ethelred, perking up a bit. 'The diamonds may never have been here. The envelope was always empty.'

I too looked from one to the other. Who knew for certain about the diamonds? Me. Ethelred. Proctor. And two out of three of us had just fibbed. I'd rejected Proctor's advances; had Ethelred sold out in the meantime?

'Very well,' I said, changing the subject. 'Who killed Davidov?'

'Oh, that's easy,' said Proctor.

'Is it?' I asked.

'Gold,' said Taylor.

'Gold,' said the Danish boy.

'But Gold was already dead,' I pointed out.

'We've said that Gold had probably brought cyanide with him and had purchased the truffles, including one of Davidov's favourites,' said Taylor. 'Gold, remember, was a pharmacist and had a good knowledge of poisons. He injects one chocolate with a massive dose of cyanide. I can't tell you which one.'

'The peach truffle,' I said, frowning. 'It was the peach truffle. His favourite.'

'Very good,' said Taylor. 'So, it is the peach truffle: the chocolate that he knows Davidov will choose first. But he is killed before he gets to give Davidov this deadly gift. What happens next? My guess is that Davidov sees the box of truffles lying there and takes them. Why? Perhaps his fingerprints are on it... or Davidov may just have fancied some truffles. Either way, the chocolates end up in his room and he leaves them untouched until the following morning. Then, needing to console himself for the loss of his envelope, he selects and eats one splendid... peach truffle.'

'That's right,' said Ethelred.

'That's right,' said Proctor.

'That's what we thought too,' said the Danish girl.

'That still doesn't make her a real detective,' said the Danish boy.

The mother smiled proudly. 'They both worked it out a long time ago,' she said.

'Yes, it was always the most likely scenario,' said the Inspector, 'though we of course needed to question everyone to rule out other possibilities. Davidov killed Gold. Then several hours later Gold killed Davidov. It really was very obvious. Unless, of course, you were perversely looking for complications that were not there. We recovered the kitchen knife, by the way—it was in the river, not thrown out with the rubbish. Since, Elsie, you removed two pieces of valuable evidence, we were unaware of the receipt and the coins, but the pattern of blood splashes on Gold's dressing gown was completely wrong for the murder victim. There was no hole in it corresponding to the slash in the pyjama jacket and to the wound. It had clearly been thrown randomly over the body after the stabbing. We were aware of the accusations that *Monsieur* Davidov was harbouring the diamonds. To be ignorant of it would mean that you had not read a newspaper for months—or only *Hello! Magazine* and the *Bookseller*. The connection was clear. Had Davidov lived he would not have stood a chance of getting away with it. It was a very amateur affair and the act of a desperate man. The poisoning was more—how would you say?—clever. The shop sells lots of truffles and strangely they did not remember Jonathan Gold. Many visitors buy their chocolates to take home. It would have been difficult to prove at what point the chocolates had been poisoned or by whom.'

'I remembered him though,' said Taylor. 'I saw him in the shop, as I told the police, though I didn't realise the significance of it until I spoke to Elsie.'

'Yes, thank you,' said the Inspector. 'That was most helpful of you, *Monsieur* Taylor. We were of course aware the cyanide was in a peach truffle because we had examined the contents of Grigory Davidov's stomach. We did not know that it was the only peach truffle, *Mademoiselle* Thirkettle, since you ate the other chocolates before we could check—so you too have been helpful in filling in one small detail.'

'So, all ten of the guests still at the hotel are innocent?' I said.

The Inspector looked up from the magazine he had started to read. 'Just so; they are all—how do you say?—little Herrings.'

'Red Herrings,' I said.

'But small ones,' he said. 'Very small ones. Ten little red Herrings. Fortunately they did not detain us long. However, I am sorry—you were going to explain, *Mademoiselle* Thirkettle, what happened to the diamonds? I am very curious to learn about this.'

'If they were ever here,' said Proctor. 'Which I somehow doubt.'

'And you, *Monsieur* Tressider, do you doubt there was anything in the envelope?' asked the Inspector.

Ethelred made a sort of choking noise which turned into a 'yes'.

'And you, *Mademoiselle* Thirkettle?'

'I certainly don't know where the diamonds are now,' I said truthfully.

'Nor me,' said Herbie.

'Nor I,' said Ethelred. I nodded at him. I always admire good grammar under pressure.

'Then how unobservant you all must be,' said the Inspector. 'Did none of you look in the little blue bag with the nice eagle—not even once? We obviously searched the railway station yesterday and found both the bag and the necklace. What we were not sure of, since *Mademoiselle* Thirkettle's story and *Monsieur* Proctor's did not quite match, was which of you had originally stolen the diamonds from the safe. You were all behaving very oddly. So we left the diamonds where they were. We deliberately let you discover that we were relaxing security and we waited to see who would leave the hotel and return to claim them. Did you notice the new CCTV camera?'

'No,' said Ethelred.

'Good—that was what we had intended. Anyway, first, two of you came along and switched the locker that they were in. Then *Monsieur* Proctor came along and was most upset to find his locker empty. Then *Monsieur* Tressider pretended to switch the diamonds to yet another locker, but put them in his pocket. I hope you enjoyed your chocolates, by the way, Mademoiselle Thirkettle.'

'You were watching us after we left the station?' I asked.

'Every step of the way,' said the Inspector. 'We would not, obviously, have wished any harm to come to you.'

'And do you know where the diamonds are now?'

'Of course,' he said.

'So where are the diamonds now?' asked Proctor glumly.

The Inspector turned to Ethelred. '*Monsieur* Tressider? Perhaps you would like to clear up this final point for us? Then we can all go home.'

Ethelred made a sort of gulping noise and his hand went instinctively for his pocket.

'Would you like to hand them over now, or would you prefer me to search you?' said the Inspector.

Ethelred reached inside his jacket pocket and removed a faded blue felt bag.

As I said, nothing could go wrong with my plan unless Ethelred was planning to behave like a moron. I watched my diamonds change hands for the last time. I felt their pain.

'Thank you,' said the Inspector.

'Hold on. Those are *my* diamonds,' said Proctor.

'We think not...unless you would like to explain?'

Herbie Proctor sighed a very long sigh and began: 'Taylor's account of events was reasonably accurate—bearing in mind he knows sod all about anything—but there was one major omission. As he said, the necklace was in the possession of the Goldsteins in the 1930s, but they were scarcely the legal owners. The Czar omitted to pay for the jewels. They remained the property of the jeweller who made then—Vladimir Borodin. Elsie asked percep-tively why the Golds didn't just go to court and argue their case. The answer is that the jewels were never rightfully theirs. They belong to the Borodin family—my clients.'

'Your clients?' asked the Inspector.

'I'm a private detective, employed by the family to recover the gems. We knew of course that Jonathan Gold was negoti-ating something quietly with Davidov and so I followed him to this hotel. We weren't sure whether his plans hadn't changed. We thought all along that he might be more interested in exacting some sort of revenge for Yacoubabad than in recovering stolen property, which would not have been good news for us.

We wanted the diamonds in London. My brief was to find out whether the necklace had changed hands, so that the Borodins could start legal action the moment the diamonds were back in the country. Alternatively—and particularly if Jonathan Gold started to do anything stupid—I was under instructions to recover the goods by direct action. If anyone was careless enough to leave them lying around.'

'They were locked in the safe,' I pointed out. 'That's hardly lying around.'

'An old hotel safe? Took me thirty seconds to discover the combination, fifteen to take out the envelope, empty it and seal it up again. Another fifteen to shut the safe door and lock it. The diamonds would have been miles away by the time Davidov discovered the loss, if it hadn't been for Jonathan Gold interfering and getting himself killed. Had I been sure he was planning to poison Davidov, I would have chanced my luck earlier. I could obviously have done without interfering busybodies like Elsie. Still, it wasn't too difficult to throw her off the scent from time to time.'

'What if Davidov had come after you?' I asked, ignoring the various insults.

Proctor nodded. 'You have indeed hit upon my biggest problem. Jonathan Gold recognised me. We were both after the same thing—and our paths had crossed before, let's say. It had always seemed likely that he or Davidov or both would put two and two together and try to have me stopped by Customs and searched—or beaten up by a couple of Davidov's goons and searched. I can't say I was keen on either option. But they wouldn't have found the diamonds on me,' he said. Herbie gave a nasty little chuckle. 'I had an infallible plan, Elsie. I was to pass the diamonds to an accomplice, who had no previous connection with any of it, who would have no knowledge of what he was smuggling into the UK, and who would ask no questions, but simply deliver the goods to me in London. Entirely free of charge.'

'What a plonker,' I said.

'Yes,' said Proctor. 'A couple of days before I came here I met up with an old friend of mine. She'd just got back from India, where she'd dumped some poor guy. When I described what I needed, she said she'd help me for…for a small cut of the profits. She'd phone this sap up and ask him to do her one small favour. She reckoned he was still so besotted with her that he'd come running with his tail wagging, however bizarre the request might be. So she instructed him to fly over and pitch up at this hotel, where somebody would contact him and give him something. He was then to deliver the goods to her at an address in London.' He turned to Ethelred and grinned.

I too turned to Ethelred. 'You silly, pointless, brain-dead tart,' I said.

The brain-dead tart said nothing, but swallowed hard.

'If he'd just stuck to his original instructions we'd have been fine,' Proctor continued. 'But Ethelred decided he'd take care of the diamonds himself—or somebody gave him fresh instructions. I always reckoned the bitch would try to cut me out if she could and that seems to be what happened—isn't it, Ethelred? He thought she'd be so grateful. Of course, once the diamonds had been handed over, that was the last he would have seen of her or the money. Bearing in mind he knew her pretty well, I can't think why he trusted her more than he trusted me. She was just using you, Ethelred. But mugs like you never learn, do they?'

'If it is any consolation, *Monsieur* Proctor, we would have recovered the diamonds whatever the two of you had done,' said the Inspector.

Proctor said nothing but scowled at the Inspector, then at Ethelred and finally at me.

'Well,' said the Inspector, 'that was most interesting. I have of course read in detective stories of gathering the suspects together in the dining room to tell them who the murderer was,

but I have never seen it done in real life. That was most infor-
mative, in the sense that it filled in one or two very minor and
unimportant details that we were a bit unsure of. I do not think,
however, that we shall make it a standard part of our procedures
in future. It was also helpful in that I effectively have confessions
from three of you that you have been involved in some way in
the theft of several million Euros in diamonds from this hotel. It
should considerably speed your convictions. I am most grateful.'

'What!' said Herbie Proctor. For once I can say that he spoke
for all of us.

The Inspector smiled. 'Just a little joke,' he said. 'You see, we
policemen do have a sense of humour, no? I am sure, in spite of
any indication that you may have given to the contrary, that it was
always the intention of all three of you to retrieve the diamonds
and return them safely to us. If that was not your intention,
then you are collectively the worst diamond thieves I have ever
encountered.'

Now I knew who Ethelred had been dealing with, I realised
that my own plan (accidentally giving away the location of the
diamonds) had been the best one after all. There was no way I
was letting that Floozy make a fool of my Ethelred. Much better
the police had the loot than she did.

'Quite right,' I said. 'That was the intention all along. I am
delighted that you now have the diamonds. Even the runt of the
litter.'

'But,' said Herbie Proctor, 'they are legally the property of
my clients.'

'And they will have the chance of arguing that in a French
court. For the moment, however,' said the Inspector, 'they are the
property of the French Government, as by the way, are the two
Pound coins that Mademoiselle Thirkettle found in the dressing
gown pocket—you may keep the restaurant receipt however as a
souvenir of your visit. It is of no possible value as evidence.'

'So that's it?' I asked.

Ethelred was still staring into space. A small tear was running down his cheek. He did nothing to wipe it away.

'The man's crying,' said the Danish girl.

'He's sad about the Indian lady,' said his mother.

I walked across the room to Ethelred and gave him a big, big hug. Well, little boys get into scrapes, but you can't stay angry with them long, can you?

'Thank you for your patience. You are all free to go,' said the Inspector, with a nod to the guests. '*La comedia e finita.*'

POSTSCRIPT

We had travelled back through misty December countryside. The fields on either side of the railway track faded away towards indistinct, spiky pollards. The land seemed irrevocably drenched, with grey sheets of water chequering the brown earth. The villages had closed in on themselves. The roads were slick and dull.

We said very little to each other between Tours and Paris; and, later, the rattle of the Metro made proper conversation impossible as we crossed the city. I was in any case worried that Elsie had left only half an hour for us to get from the Gare St Lazare to the Gare du Nord. I spent much of the journey looking at the map, counting stations, multiplying minutes. In the end, we arrived in plenty of time—a fact that, for some unknown reason, amused Elsie greatly—and had settled into our seats well before the London train departed.

We travelled on in silence through the bleak Paris suburbs, with the rain still falling miserably. As we crossed the dreary, flat lands of the Pas de Calais, hail rattled against the windows. It was only when we were through the tunnel and travelling across Kent that the sun broke through the clouds. And it was at that point that I again raised the question that had been on my mind since the phone call.

'What did you mean about my being dead?' I demanded.

Elsie looked slightly embarrassed. 'Did I say that? Surely not?'

'You said it more than once. What did you do: have me declared legally dead?'

'Oh, no,' she said. 'Not that exactly.'

'What, exactly?'

She took a deep breath. 'You remember that you left a manuscript for me to get published?'

'I left a manuscript. I told you that I was rather relieved you hadn't read it. A lot of it was very personal. It wasn't intended for publication or anything. Not even you would have gone ahead and...'

'The launch party is tonight at Goldsboro Books.'

'But...' I said.

I tried to remember what was in the final draft. It concerned a previous investigation that I had conducted with Elsie and I had admitted to doing a number of things that were less than one hundred percent legal. And as far as my relations with women were concerned...

'I'm going to look a total prat,' I said. 'And I'll probably get arrested. Did you publish it exactly as I wrote it?'

'Of course not,' she said, 'I added a few bits of my own.'

'And what did you say?' My heart would have sunk, but it was already as low as it could get.

'I changed the ending a bit.'

'How much?'

'You die in a plane crash on your way to join your floozy. There's a bomb on your plane. I am stricken with grief, but only for a very short time.'

'But I didn't die in a plane crash.'

'You deserved to,' she said, as if it were all my fault.

I thought about this. She was right. I deserved to. But I hadn't.

'So at the book launch tonight,' I said, 'I shall get arrested for wasting police time, for...'

'No you won't,' said Elsie confidently.

'Why?'

'I turned it into fiction,' she said. 'I even changed your name—and a few other facts.'

'What did you call me?' I asked.

'Ethelred Tressider,' she said.

'Well, that's marginally better than my real name,' I said. 'What did you call yourself?'

'Elsie Thirkettle,' said 'Elsie Thirkettle'.

'That's marginally better than *your* real name,' I said.

'There you are, then.'

'Even so...' I said.

'We could use the names again for a sequel,' she said.

'There will be no sequel. I'm not doing sequels.'

'Oh come on, "Ethelred",' said 'Elsie'. 'I really got into this joint authorship business. We could write about a double murder in a place I'll call "Chaubord". I'll do the first chapter.'

'Absolutely no way,' I said. 'Also, stop doing that thing with your fingers.'

'Please. We'll change some facts in that one too—you'll be quite safe.'

'No.'

'Please, please, please.'

'No.'

'I'll tell the police what really happened,' said Elsie.

I realised then that your heart can always sink just that little bit more.

'Very well,' I said, 'but I'm not trusting you to write the final chapter. Not after last time. I'm not getting killed again.'

She gave this a bit of thought. 'OK—you write the last chapter. I take it I can trust you not to try to get some sort of childish revenge?'

Sadly, before I could reply, the automatic doors hissed open and a weasely individual marched into the carriage, clutching a Walther P99 semi-automatic.

'You've had this coming to you,' snarled Herbie Proctor.

Two shots rang out, and Elsie slumped back, limp and lifeless, into her seat.

Well, that would teach *her* to mess with metafiction.

Outside, the English countryside slipped effortlessly by in the bright winter sunshine. Long shadows snaked across the rich, oily furrows. From the chimney of a distant thatched cottage, a thin, pearl grey thread of wood smoke rose into the blue sky. Everything was tranquil and calm.

It was, after all, going to be a fine evening. I began to look forward to the book launch.

Want more Ethelred and Elsie?
See how it all began with

The Herring Seller's Apprentice

nominated for a
2010 Edgar Award for Best Paperback Original.

(read on for sample of first chapter)

CHAPTER 1

I have always been a writer.

I wrote my first novel at the age of six. It was seven and a half pages long and concerned a penguin, who happened to have the same name as me, and a lady hedgehog, who happened to have the same name as my schoolteacher. After overcoming some minor difficulties and misunderstandings they became firm friends and lived happily ever after; but their relationship was, understandably, entirely platonic. At the age I was then, hedgehog-meets-penguin struck me as a plot with greater possibilities than boy-meets-girl.

Little has changed. Today I am three writers and none of us seems to be able to write about sex.

Perhaps for that reason, none of us is especially successful. Together, we just about make a living, but we do not appear on the best-seller lists in the *Sunday Times*. We do not give readings at Hay-on-Wye. The British Council does not ask us to undertake tours of sub-Saharan Africa or to be writer in residence at Odense University. We do not win the Costa Prize for anything.

I am not sure that I like any of me but, of the three choices available, I have always been most comfortable being Peter Fielding. Peter Fielding writes crime novels featuring the redoubtable Sergeant Fairfax of the Buckfordshire Police. Fairfax is in late middle age and much embittered by his lack of promotion and by my inability to write him sex of any kind. When I first invented him, sixteen years ago, he was fifty-eight and about to be prematurely retired. He is now fifty-eight and a half and has solved twelve almost impossible cases in the intervening six months. He is probably quite justified in believing that he has been unfairly passed over.

Under the pen-name of J. R. Elliot I also write historical crime novels. I am not sure of J. R. Elliot's gender, but increasingly I think that I may be female. The books are all set in the reign of Richard II because I can no longer be bothered to research any other period. It is a well-established fact that nobody had sex between 1377 and 1399.

As Amanda Collins I produce an easily readable 150 pages of romantic fiction every eight months or so, to a set style and a set formula provided by the publisher. Miss Collins is popular with ladies of limited imagination and little experience of the real world. A short study of the genre had already revealed to me that doctors were the heroes of much romantic fiction—usually they were GPs or heart surgeons. I decided to choose the relatively obscure specialty of oral and maxillofacial surgery for mine. Oral and maxillofacial surgeons have a great deal of sex, occasionally with their own wives. But they do so very discreetly. My ladies prefer it that way, and so do I. The three of us share an agent: Ms Elsie Thirkettle. She is the only person I have ever met, under the age of seventy, named Elsie. I once asked her, in view of the unfashionableness of her first name, and the fact that she clearly has no great love of it, why she didn't use her second name.

She looked at me as if I were an idiot boy that she had been tricked into babysitting by unkind neighbours. 'Do I look like a sodding Yvette?'

'But why did your parents call you Elsie, Elsie?'

'They never did like me. Tossers, the pair of them.'

My parents did not like me either. They called me Ethelred.

My father's assurance that I was named after King Ethelred I (866–871) and not Ethelred the Unready (978–1016) was little consolation to a seven-year-old whose friends all called him 'Ethel'. I experimented with introducing myself as 'Red' for a while, but for some reason it never did catch on amongst my acquaintances. Oh, and my second name is Hengist, in case you were about to ask. Ethelred Hengist Tressider. It has never surprised anyone that I might prefer to be known as Amanda Collins.

It is possible that all agents despise authors, in the same way that school bursars despise headmasters, head waiters despise diners, chefs despise head waiters and shop assistants despise shoppers. Few agents despise authors quite so openly as Elsie, however.

'Authors? Couldn't fart without an agent to remind them where their arses are.'

I rarely try to contradict remarks of this sort. Based on Elsie's other clients, this is fair comment. Many of them probably could not fart even given this thoughtful assistance.

Elsie does in fact represent quite a number of other authors as well as the three of me. Occasionally we ask each other why we have settled for this loud, plump, eccentrically dressed little woman, who claims to enjoy neither the company of writers nor literature of any kind. Has she deliberately gathered together a group of particularly weak-willed individuals who lack the spirit either to answer her back or to leave her? Or do we all secretly enjoy having our work and our characters abused? Neither answer is convincing. The real reason is painful but quite clear: none of us is terribly good and Elsie is very successful at selling our manuscripts. She is also very honest in her criticism of our work.

'It's crap.'

'Would you like to be more specific?'

'It's dog's crap.'

'I see.' I fingered the manuscript on the table between us.

Just the first draft of the first few chapters, but I had rather hoped that it would be universally hailed as a masterpiece.

'Leave the literary crime novel to Barbara sodding Vine. You can't do it. She can. Or, to put it another way, she can, you can't. Is that specific enough for you or would you like me to embroider it for you on a tea cosy in cross stitch?'